Gillian's Heart

By

B J Bassett

D1736386

Dedication

In loving memory of my friend, Judy. I miss you.

And to my cheerleaders, Debbie and Jennie.

Acknowledgements

There were many who contributed to the writing of *Gillian's Heart*. Thank you for your critiques: Sharon Brown, Nick Harrison, Jean Murray, Deanna Enos, Christine Sackey, Bonnie Leon, Ann Shorey, Billy Cook, Julia Ewert, Diane L. Goeres-Gardner and Sarah Schartz.

Thank you Laura Hilton, Kathleen Frisen, Julie Arduini, Christy Miller, Joi Copeland, Penny McGinnis, Heidi Kortman, and Joann Kirby for fine-tuning the manuscript.

I am grateful to Editor-In-Chief Gail Delaney and staff at Desert Breeze Publishing, Inc. for their expertise, essential to originally publishing of *Gillian's Heart*.

With love and appreciation to my daughter Melanie for her ideas and encouragement, and my husband Ed who always supports my endeavors.

Table of Contents

Chapter One

Baggy pink sweats concealed Gillian Grant's ninety-pound skeletal body as she tramped through the wet grass to the edge of the cliff. She raised the American flag just as her grandmother had done every morning since the Vietnam War. Gillian had taken on the flag raising ritual after Gram's passing. She gazed over the Pacific through the June fog. It cloaked the majestic ocean like Gillian's fears ensconced her heart.

Her grandmother's Cape Cod style beach cottage on Cliff Drive in Reagan Beach was once a well-kept home. Now it was weathered from the hot southern California sun. The home had been in the Stewart family since 1958, and it needed as much tenderness as the family itself.

Gillian trudged over the dew covered lawn and climbed the rickety stairs to the apartment above the detached garage. She walked through the bedroom, bath, and combination living room and kitchen, giving the apartment one last inspection. *Not bad if I do say so myself.* She grabbed the caddy with rags, brushes, and cleaning solvents. In the other hand, she carried a bottle of bleach, and descended the stairs. She stowed the cleaning supplies in the laundry room of the main house and entered the kitchen.

Samantha, Gillian's best friend, sat at the kitchen table.

Gillian poured a cup of hot water, slipped a chamomile tea bag in it, and joined Samantha in the little kitchenette with the large window overlooking the Pacific. "The apartment is finally ready." Gillian sighed.

Samantha shivered in her white t-shirt and red plaid Joe Boxers. She tightened her grip on the mug of hazelnut coffee and flexed her feet in the fluffy pink slippers. "When are Josh and his friend supposed to get here?" She yawned.

"Any time."

Samantha cocked her head. "Did Josh say anything more about his friend?"

"His name is Dusty and he met him in Santa Cruz."

Gillian sipped her tea, remembering the aroma of mornings with Gram. She sighed. "I can't believe it's been three months since Gram died." She nibbled at a bran muffin, digging the raisins out and lining them in a row like they were playing follow the leader. "Do you think I'm doing the right thing, renting the apartment to a stranger? Gram was always so careful about who she rented to."

Samantha smiled. "Josh isn't a stranger. He's more like a brother."

"He's bringing a stranger with him. What if?"

Samantha flipped her hair behind her ear. "Look, Gilly, the only way you can afford this place is to rent the apartment. Have you forgotten you need the money? I'm sure Josh's friend isn't an ax murderer, or rapist, or stalker, or whatever. Give Josh some credit."

"I know, I guess I'm being paranoid." She looked out the kitchenette window at the ocean. "You're right. Besides the income for the property taxes, the house needs so much work. I need to remind myself why I decided not to teach summer school. I have to put Gram's affairs in order and repair the house."

"With me renting your spare room and Josh and his friend renting the apartment, you're becoming a regular landlord." She leaned across the table towards Gillian and whispered, "You know I've always had a crush on Josh."

Gillian grinned. "Who don't you have a crush on?"

"What can I say? It's who I am."

They sipped their warm drinks.

"Cleaning the apartment last night wiped me out," Gillian said. "I think I'm going to relax today."

"While you're lounging around, I'll head over to Mom and Dad's to pack the rest of my stuff."

"Great." *Without the rent money from Sam, I could lose Gram's house.*

The faint rattle of an old vehicle grew louder as it came closer to the weed-lined driveway.

Samantha jumped from her seat, almost spilling her coffee. "They're here! I better get presentable."

When she returned, they peeked out from behind the white sheer Priscilla crisscrossed curtains.

Behind Josh's old Honda stood a tall, broad-shouldered man with curly hair, too long for Gillian's taste.

"He must be Dusty," Gillian whispered. He came around to the front of a red '65 Mustang with several surfboards on top, and towing a small U-Haul trailer. His worn tank top, faded cut offs, and frayed flip flops meant one thing.

"Oh great, a surfer," Gillian said, then added under her breath, "I wonder how much work I'll get out of him?" A lump caught in her throat. *What am I getting myself into?* She straightened and untwisted her grimace. "Let's go meet my new handyman, Sam."

They went outside to greet the new renters.

Standing in the middle of the driveway, Josh, a stocky redhead with freckles, enveloped Gillian in a bear hug. His strength made her sigh with relief. Before releasing her, he whispered in her ear, "I'm sorry about your grandmother."

With her arms still around his neck, incessant tears puddled her eyes. "Thanks." She pressed down the despair. She knew when her chest tightened and her breath quickened, she must push it away like the waves expel rocks.

Josh released Gillian. "Hey Sam, long time no see."

"Hi, Josh." Samantha clasped her hands behind her. She swayed from side to side.

"Gillian Grant and Samantha Peterson, meet Dusty Bradshaw." Josh patted Dusty on the back.

Dusty grinned. "What a great place."

Gillian stared. *The purr of his voice and gentleness of his eyes don't do a thing for me. He's just another surfer.*

"It needs a lot of work," Gillian said. "My grandmother couldn't afford to keep the place maintained, so almost everything needs repairs." There was an awkward silence, and then Gillian said, "Would you like to see the apartment?"

"You bet." Dusty clapped his hands like a boy ready to get into the game.

Gillian led the way to the stairs on the outside of the garage. "I've been cleaning." They strolled through the combination living room and kitchen to the hall. Dusty poked his head into the bedroom.

"It's only a one bedroom," Gillian apologized, as she pushed a stray strand of hair off her forehead.

Josh peered over Dusty's shoulder into the bedroom. "At least it has twin beds." He nodded toward Dusty. "I'm not sleeping in the same bed with him."

"The feeling's mutual." Dusty grinned

Gillian laughed. "Do you want to see the beach?"

"Just what Dusty's been waiting for." Josh rubbed his hands together appearing eager to get going.

They descended the sagging wooden stairs to the beach.

Josh held his hands out as he gazed at the beach. "Didn't I tell you this was a surfer's paradise?"

"I'm sold." Dusty smiled at Gillian.

She returned his smile knowing hers wasn't genuine, but more like the indifference of an economics professor.

"Josh said you have experience in construction and you'd be willing to do the necessary repairs around here in exchange for your share of the rent."

"Yeah, I can help you out," Dusty said.

Gillian bristled at his words. *Help me out? I'm not a charity case.* "I'll show you what needs to be done. And you can tell me if you can do them."

"Lead the way." Dusty bowed and gestured with his arm like she was royalty.

Could he be any more annoying? Gillian chafed. *I'll show him who's boss.*

They climbed the stairs from the beach as Gillian laid everything out. "As you can see, the stairs going down to the beach need repair...and there's the gardening. Everything needs pruning, and the driveway needs to be replaced or resurfaced." She nodded toward the peeling paint. "The house needs to be painted. I'll paint the inside, but the exterior needs paint too." Gillian took a breath. It was unnerving her to recount all the jobs and avoid Dusty's eyes at the same time. "Come on in the house."

They sat in the kitchen. Gillian placed a renter's agreement on the table in front of them. "I've already explained the agreement to Josh. I'll rent the apartment at a reduced rate in exchange for repairs done to the property. Your half of the rent will be waived as long as you're working on the house. Understood?"

"Yes ma'am."

"Can you do the work?" She indicated to Dusty with the end of her pen.

"Sure can. I've been working in construction for the last several years."

"Do you have references?"

Dusty reached in his back pocket and pulled out a worn paper. Placing it on the table in front of her, he smoothed out the folds. "I thought you'd ask."

Gillian eyed the crumpled resume. "I'll be calling them."

Dusty grinned. "I'm sure you will."

"School starts in two and a half months and I'd like most of the work done by then. Is it possible?" Gillian asked.

"I don't see why not."

Josh had sat patiently during the discourse between the two and eagerly nodded. He put his hand on Dusty's shoulder. "So what do you think?"

Gillian felt Dusty's penetrating hazel eyes on her.

"Is the use of the beach part of the deal?" Dusty asked.

"Yes."

Dusty reached for a pen. "You've got a deal. Where do I sign?"

After Dusty and Josh signed the rental agreement, Josh handed Gillian his portion of the rent in cash. "When can we move in?"

"Now, if you want," Gillian said.

4

Josh shoved back the maple kitchen chair from the table. "Then let's get started. Welcome to Reagan Beach, Dusty." He stood. "Hey. I've got a great idea! How about going out for pizza tonight?"

Samantha looked at Gillian. "Sounds good to me."

"I'm in." Dusty said.

Gillian thought a moment. "I don't know... I have to go over my Sunday school lesson for tomorrow."

"Come on, Gilly. Don't be a party pooper." Samantha's eyebrows arched in appeal.

"Okay, I'll go."

Gillian and Samantha ushered Dusty and Josh to the front door.

Dusty stopped and turned to Gillian. "Can I store my surfboards in the garage?"

"Okay."

"Me too?" Josh asked.

"Of course."

Samantha laughed. "Just another perk of living here."

"What a great landlord." Josh brushed a kiss across Gillian's cheek. "Pick you up at six."

Josh and Dusty headed toward their vehicles to unload and move in.

Gillian and Samantha returned to the kitchenette. Soon the fog dissolved, and Gillian felt the warm sun caress her back as it streamed through the window.

Samantha smiled. "What do you think?"

"About what?"

Samantha wadded up a napkin and threw it at Gillian. "Not what. Who, silly. What do you think of Dusty?"

"He seems too..."

"Too what?"

"Sure of himself."

"What's wrong with being confident?" Samantha cocked her head to one side.

Gillian was more concerned about the arrangements she had made with a perfect stranger than discussing him. Sure Dusty was tall, tanned, and muscular. And his curly dark hair reminded her of what Samson in the Bible must have looked like. She saw the man all the girls undoubtedly swooned over, but thought he'd probably be a big disappointment. Was brawn and looks all there was to him?

Gillian's silence did not deter Samantha. "Some people don't make good first impressions."

"Well, Dusty Bradshaw didn't make a good first impression on me."

5

"He did me."

Gillian poured another cup of tea. "He's okay, I guess."

"What do you mean, okay? You've got to be kidding! He's gorgeous. His eyes. His muscles. His tan. His smile. I'm in love." Samantha left the kitchen, waltzed into the living room, and collapsed on the sofa.

"You sound like a teenager."

Samantha closed her eyes. "I don't care what I sound like. I'm definitely looking forward to tonight."

Gillian sipped her tea. *Oh, Samantha, what fantasies are whirling around in your mind?*

Chapter Two

Dusty stowed a beach chair next to his surfboards in the garage. Before returning to his car in the driveway, he closed his eyes and breathed deeply. A whiff of the familiar salty air made him think of Pop. *Not now. I can't think about him now.*

Josh lifted a heavy box out of his trunk and hoisted it to his shoulder. "So, what do you think of Gillian?"

"The lady's uptight."

"Uptight!" Josh scowled.

"She doesn't seem like the person you described."

"She's changed." Josh groaned under the weight of the box.

Dusty grabbed a load of clothes and wrapped them over his arm and followed Josh up the stairs. He took the steps two at a time, avoiding the exposed nails. After hanging the clothes in the closet, he entered the living room where Josh sat on the couch.

Josh ran his hand through his red hair. "Sorry for jumping down your throat. It's just... she's had a rough life. Her mother and stepfather are alcoholics and they abandoned her. When they did come around, it was only to get money from Gillian's grandmother and then they'd leave again." He stood and paced. "I'd probably be uptight too if I'd had parents like hers. Gillian's great. You'll just have to get to know her."

"I'm sure I will. It seems she's not only my landlord, but my boss too."

"I'm worried about her."

Dusty sensed Josh's concern. He sat down on the couch, his forearms rested on his thighs, hands clasped. "What about?"

"She's too thin. When I hugged her, there was nothing there."

"Do you think there's something wrong with her?"

"Like what?" Josh scratched his head.

"Could she have an eating disorder?"

"You mean like anorexia?"

"Yeah. Maybe."

Josh ambled toward the open door. "What if she isn't eating because she's grieving?"

Dusty followed him through the doorway and down the stairs. "Or it could be as simple as dieting. You know how women like to be thin."

"Sure."

Although Josh agreed with him, Dusty didn't think Josh sounded convincing.

7

Dusty pitched his clothes in drawers and set up the entertainment center. He was desperate to be in the water and glide through the waves, but he owed it to Josh to be nice to Gillian. So he tugged at the snarls in his hair, smoothed his shirt, and decided to try to see in Gillian what Josh saw.

By six o'clock sharp, they had both showered, shaved, and were at Gillian's front door. Gillian opened the door wearing a white sleeveless blouse, her jeans hung on her hipless body.

"Are the fair maidens ready to devour a famous pizza at BJ's?" Josh asked. "Dusty's car is nicer than mine, to say the least, so he's driving."

"Shotgun!" Samantha squealed as she sprinted, beating the others to Dusty's car.

Dusty opened the passenger door and pushed the leather seat up for Gillian to slide into the backseat. He caught a whiff of the fragrance she wore. *Nice. Not too much, fresh.* He slid behind the wheel.

From the backseat, Josh tapped Dusty on the shoulder. "Take a left at the highway."

"Hey, Sam, remember the time you puked on my dad's sailboat?" Josh said.

Samantha groaned. "Don't remind me." She turned to face Gillian and Josh in the backseat. "What about the time, at Hume Lake, when you put Vaseline on the toilet seat and Pastor Mike sat on it, Josh?" Samantha teased. "Or the time Joe Muster poured a bucket of ice water over your head in the shower."

"How'd you know about it?" Josh asked.

Samantha winked at Gillian. "Oh, we gals have our ways."

Dusty enjoyed their banter. Laughter from the backseat caused him to glance in the rear-view mirror and catch a glimpse of Gillian's radiant smile. *She doesn't appear to be the same edgy gal I met earlier today. Maybe Josh is right about her.*

Josh's voice jarred Dusty from his thoughts. "Make a right at the next street."

*****

Gillian and the others followed the hostess to an open booth and the girls scooted into one side of it. After perusing the menu, they ordered.

The waitress returned with soft drinks and placed them around the table.

Josh rambled, "I went to college, got a history degree, and the only job I can find is selling dental supplies. What was I thinking?"

Gillian twirled the straw around in her diet Pepsi. "You could become a teacher someday."

"I'd have to get a teaching degree and then student teach for a year." Josh shook his head. "I've had enough of school. It took me ten years to get this far."

Dusty leaned back in the booth. "In this economy, you're probably just glad to have a job."

Josh brightened. "It has its perks. I pick up my company car on Monday."

Gillian looked across the table at Dusty. "What kind of a job are you looking for, Dusty?"

"Construction, but there's no hurry. I've got plenty of work to do at your place, right?"

"Yeah." Gillian sipped her diet Pepsi and glanced through the window. *What is he doing here? He seems out of place. Like he's lost.*

Samantha flipped her hair behind her ear. "So how did you guys meet?"

"Surfing." Dusty set his drink aside and leaned closer. "We were sitting on surfboards, waiting for a wave in Santa Cruz. We started talking and discovered we have a lot of things in common."

"Like what?" Samantha sipped her drink.

"Surfing." Both Dusty and Josh said at the same time.

Gillian unfolded and refolded her paper napkin. "How come you left Santa Cruz?"

"My mother got married," Dusty said. "I wanted to give the newlyweds some privacy. Besides, it was time I got out on my own."

Gillian picked at her pepperoni pizza. Something about what he said sounded so familiar. He had a home, but not really. *Did he feel like he was in the way?* She remembered a time when she felt abandoned, but then there was Gram and the beach house. She smiled at Dusty for the first time since meeting him.

Dusty wiped his mouth with a napkin. "My dad died before I was born, so it's just been my mom and me and... my grandfather, but he's gone now too. My mom and I are close, but it was time for me to leave. So -- here I am."

Samantha raised her glass. "I propose a toast. Josh has come back home, Gillian's a landlord, and Dusty and I have moved out on our own. Here's to new beginnings... and to friendship." They clicked each other's glasses.

After finishing the pizza, Josh pushed away from the table, covered in a massacre of greasy napkins and pizza crust, and patted his belly. "How about going over to Balboa to the amusement park?"

Samantha jumped up. "Sounds great."

*****

9

Gillian and Samantha waited inside the theme park while Dusty and Josh purchased tickets at the booth. It was a balmy night without the usual June fog rolling in. Gillian reminisced about the happy memories she spent here with Samantha and Josh and their youth group. *I wonder if tonight will be memorable.*

The guys approached them, Josh holding a fist full of tickets fanned out like it was a bouquet. "What's your pleasure?"

Gillian and Samantha looked at each other and blurted in unison, "The bumper cars."

Josh handed the attendant the tickets and Samantha and Gillian burst through the gate and climbed into a dented red car. Gillian took the seat behind the steering wheel, Samantha slid in next to her. Dusty chose a blue car and Josh nabbed a bright yellow one. When the ride began, Gillian felt daring and steered her car between the guys' cars.

Samantha turned around and squealed, "Faster, Gilly, faster. Here they come!"

Gillian felt the jolt when Dusty bumped her and her car spun around, headed in the opposite direction, and Josh plowed into her. With her car out of control and going in circles, Dusty rammed them again before Gillian was able to get her car going in the right direction. Gillian screamed and giggled and felt a freedom she hadn't felt in months.

When the ride ended, Gillian watched Josh leap out of his car. *I'm so glad he's home.*

They left the ride laughing and then strolled toward the arcade. After playing some pinball machines, they came outside again and threw baseballs at milk bottles. Samantha, Gillian, and Josh knocked some bottles down, but it was Dusty who won the stuffed pink dog.

"Here." Dusty handed it to Samantha.

Samantha clutched the plush animal. "Thanks."

They ambled through the amusement park. Samantha darted ahead. "Let's ride the Ferris wheel."

Samantha slid onto the seat. Before Gillian could sit next to her, Josh pulled her back. "We'll take the next one." Josh pushed Dusty toward Samantha.

Gillian and Josh waited for the next empty seat. She was glad she'd be able to spend some time alone with him -- comfortable Josh, safe Josh. *Let Samantha have the handsome hunk. I'm with Josh.*

Once up in the air, Josh turned to her. "Gillian I'm worried about you. Is something wrong?"

"What do you mean?"

"You did everything with your pizza tonight, except eat it."

"I ate it!"

"You picked at it!"

10

"We gals like to watch our figures."

"You're too thin."

"I like being thin." She folded her arms across her chest.

"Gillian--" Josh sounded defeated.

*****

The four left the amusement park and rode back to Reagan Beach. Samantha hugged her stuffed toy close to her as she chattered. The others were quiet. Gillian wondered if they were lost in their own thoughts as she was in hers, like boats at sea. *What does Josh mean -- I'm too thin? He's changed. He's not the old fun, comfortable, safe Josh. I'm glad he has to go to work tomorrow. Then I'll only have to deal with Dusty. Ugh!*

Later, in the living room, Gillian wrapped herself in the warm afghan. Gram had knitted the pattern of yellow roses for Gillian's sixteenth birthday. She opened her Bible and teacher's guide and reviewed her Sunday school lesson.

Samantha strolled through the living room where Gillian sat. "Wasn't it a great evening?"

"It was fine."

"What's the matter?"

"Nothing." Gillian tried to concentrate on her lesson. She narrowed her eyes and reread the introduction.

"Didn't you have a good time?"

"It was all right."

"Well, did you or didn't you?"

Gillian looked up with exasperation. "Sam, I'm trying to go over my lesson."

"I'm confused. You were having fun until... until you and Josh went on the Ferris wheel together."

"I was."

"Well, what happened?"

"We had a disagreement."

"No way! You, the people pleaser, disagreed with Josh?"

"Sam, it's late and I really need to review my lesson and get to bed."

"Gillian Grant, do you mean to tell me you're going to make me wait until tomorrow to find out what you and Josh argued about?"

"I don't want to talk about it."

Samantha waited.

Gillian kept her eyes fixed on her Bible. "Good night, Samantha."

"Night, Gilly." Samantha shuffled away in her bunny slippers, grumbling to herself.

Chapter Three

Gillian tossed and turned and tossed some more. Memories crowded her mind. Memories of her mother's nagging voice. *Pack your things. You have to go.* "Oh Lord, I must get some sleep. Please help me." Sleep didn't come and the hours continued to tick away. Her head pounded. *If Gram were here, she'd stroke my hair and know exactly what to say.*

Gillian had never told anyone, not even Samantha, about talking to her grandmother, especially on sleepless nights like this one. "Gram, I miss you so much." Gillian rolled over on her side and hugged her pillow. "I miss our time together -- just the two of us. I miss seeing you working in the garden and in the kitchen. I miss our evenings reading and watching you knit. I miss seeing you sitting with your head resting on the back of your chair, listening to me play the piano. How can I go on without you?"

She turned over on her back again, and through her tears, she stared up at the dark ceiling. "Gram, what've I done letting a stranger move into the apartment? I don't like anyone in our home. I'm not sure I even like Josh and Samantha living here. I miss our peaceful little home with just you and me. Oh, Gram, Gram, what have I done?" Gillian turned onto her stomach, buried her face into the pillow, and sobbed.

After she had no more tears to cry, she turned onto her back. *Maybe if I recite the Bible memory verse for my class it will help.* "Trust in the Lord with all your heart. Lean not on your own understanding. In all your ways acknowledge him and he will direct your paths," she quoted from memory. "Oh, Father, I must, I must put my trust in you. Please help me."

Early Sunday morning, Gillian made her pilgrimage to the edge of the cliff and raised the flag. "For you, Gram." She glanced over the edge of the cliff and saw Dusty all alone, sitting on his surfboard in the calm water, waiting for a wave. Gram had always loved watching the surfers. She would say they were at peace. *Dusty, are you at peace I wonder? I don't have time to think about Dusty.* Gillian returned to the house and dressed for church.

She glanced in the mirror. *A size three and I still look fat! I don't care if Josh thinks I'm thin. So what if I find my clothes in the children's department. I like wearing a size three. What's with him? I know women who are size 2 and even 1.*

A yellow linen jacket over the pastel print dress completed her outfit. Her thick brown hair fell into a smooth hair style with wispy bangs.

*****

Gillian carried the vase full of fresh cut roses into her Sunday school classroom. She placed them on a low table next to an open Bible and an offering basket. She greeted her first student with a smile and a pat on the shoulder. "Good morning, Bobby."

Her class went well with only one snag, when Matthew pushed Sarah out of her chair. Gillian brought the class back under control, and consoled Sarah with a hug.

When Sunday school was over and she had the classroom in order, she headed toward the sanctuary with her music clutched close to her. She arranged her sheet music on the piano and began to play a medley of hymns as the small church by the sea filled with worshipers. Just before the service began, she noticed Josh come down the side aisle. She mouthed the words, "Where's Sam?"

Josh shrugged and took a seat in the front row, next to the piano.

Gillian smiled when Pastor Mike announced, "Glad to have you back with us, Josh."

She wiped the perspiration from her palms on her dress before she placed her fingers on the keys to play the offertory. She had practiced the arrangement for the past week, until she could play it without any mistakes. Asking God to glorify Himself with the music, she began to play "Fairest Lord Jesus," first softly and slowly, then building to a crescendo at the end. When she had finished, she exhaled. She no longer cringed at all the mistakes, realizing no one heard them, except her. The congregation applauded as she took her seat next to Josh.

Pastor Mike stepped to the pulpit. "Thank you, Gillian, for the lovely rendition of 'Fairest Lord Jesus'. God has blessed you with a talent and you bring honor to Him every Sunday with it." He smiled at Gillian then he began to preach on forgiveness.

Gillian tried to listen to the sermon, but her mind kept wandering away. *Where's Sam?* She mentally shook herself back to the message only to be lost in thought again. *It feels good sitting next to Josh, feeling his arm brush mine. He smells clean, crisp.* She loved him like the brother she never had.

After the service, Gillian stood beside Josh as members clustered around them, inundating him with questions. When they were able to break away, she asked, "I'm worried about Sam. Have you seen her?"

He shook his head.

"It's not like her to miss church. I hope she's okay."

"I'm sure she's fine."

Gillian rummaged around in her purse, looking for her cell phone. "I'm going to call her."

Samantha answered on the third ring.

"You okay?" Gillian asked, unable to bridle the fear in her voice.

"I decided to play hooky."

Gillian sighed with relief. "Sam, I was worried about you."

"Don't worry, Gilly."

Gillian heard a voice in the background. "Who's there?

"Dusty." Samantha giggled.

Gillian frowned, "Well... I'll see you...when...I get home...I guess." She turned to Josh. "She's at home."

"Is she sick?"

"No. She decided to play hooky!"

"We both know she won't go to hell for playing hooky from church once in a while."

"You're right. It's just... it's not like her."

Josh rubbed his stomach. "How about a deli sandwich at Ruby's?"

Gillian stared into space, deep in thought. *So Sam played hooky. With Dusty?*

He gripped her shoulders. "Oh Josh to Gillian."

"What?"

"I'm starving. You want to grab lunch at Ruby's?"

"Sounds good."

"I'll meet you there."

They parted and soon rejoined at Ruby's. They sat at a table for two in the middle of the café, and searched the menu. After ordering, Josh, with his elbows on the table, leaned toward Gillian. "Before any more time passes, I want you to know how sorry I am I wasn't here when your grandmother died."

"It's okay." She smiled and tilted her head, as she reached out and touched his hand.

"I hope you know I'd have been here if I hadn't been a poor struggling student."

"I know. Your text messages meant a lot to me." She looked in his eyes. It was hard to steady her gaze when she felt the tears forming, but she wanted him to know it was okay.

Gillian waited while the waitress placed a tumbler of iced tea in front of her and a Coke in front of Josh. After the waitress left, Gillian continued, "It was awful watching Gram waste away those last few months." With moist eyes Gillian told him some details. She knew to stay away from her heart, the depth of despair. "Gram never

14

complained, but I knew she was in a lot of pain. The chemotherapy was horrible, and she lost her beautiful white hair. It was so sad."

"You must miss her a lot." When their order arrived, Josh salted his fries. "Did your mother and her husband come to the funeral?"

"Nope."

He paused with the salt shaker in midair. "So you made all the funeral arrangements by yourself?"

She sipped her iced tea and nodded. "I know Gram's in heaven." Gillian took a deep breath, trying to corral her emotions. "I know I'll see her again someday." She believed what she was saying, but her heart ached without end. No one, not even Josh, could fathom losing the only human love she'd ever known.

Before taking a bite of her veggie sandwich, she looked into his eyes. "So, tell me about you."

"I'll be on the road all next week with my district manager. My territory is all of California and part of Nevada."

"Do you think you're going to like being a salesman?"

"Not really. It's a way to pay off my school loans until something better comes along." He finished his burger. "Something happened to me in Santa Cruz. I don't know where to begin, so I'll just start." He wadded his napkin on his plate. "I went to a support group."

Gillian listened.

"It was called Adult Children of Alcoholics -- ACA."

"I don't understand. Your parents aren't alcoholics." Holding her sandwich in one hand, she picked out the sprouts and piled them on the plate. "They were always there for you."

"Yes and no. Physically yes, but emotionally my dad was never there. He was a workaholic." He slouched down in the chair and folded his arms. "He never took me fishing, camping, or to a ball game. He was always working or playing golf. I don't blame him for who he is or for what we never had together. I just knew I needed to let it out and move on with my life. At ACA I was able to talk to other people who shared my pain." He searched her questioning eyes. "It's a 12-Step program, and it's really helping me."

He reached across the table and put his hand over hers. "I think an ACA program would help you deal with your mother and step-father's alcoholism."

She slid her hand away and folded her arms. "I'm glad a support group helped you, but I don't need one. My mother's been gone for a long time. And anyway, I had Gram."

"You're in denial. It had to have affected you."

She crumpled her napkin on the table. "I think it's time to leave."

Josh looked defeated. "I'll pay the check."

She grabbed her purse. "Then I'll leave the tip." She folded a couple of ones, tucked them under her plate, and left as Josh paid the check.

Chapter Four

Gillian pulled her yellow VW bug into the driveway. Samantha, dressed in hot pink short shorts, carried two tumblers toward the front patio between the house and the garage. Dusty sat shirtless at the picnic table.

Gillian parked her car in the garage and grabbed her purse, Bible, and Sunday school supplies. She slammed the car door behind her.

Samantha raised the glasses. "Gilly, you want some iced tea?"

"No, thank you." Gillian knew her voice sounded curt as she rushed toward the house.

Once inside the house, she dumped her things in the den and rushed upstairs to her bedroom to change. She kicked off her shoes and freed herself from her panty hose. Soon she was dressed in shorts and a T-shirt.

Gillian nestled into her bed with a pillow propped behind her head. She picked up a book from the bedside table and tried to get interested in it, but her mind wandered. *Why do I feel like this? Why do I care if Samantha didn't go to church? Why does it hurt when Josh says I'm too thin, or thinks I should go to a support group? I'm fine.*

With her thoughts churning, Gillian had no idea what she'd just read. So she turned back to the page where she'd started and tried to concentrate on the story.

A knock at her bedroom door startled her.

"Can I come in?" Samantha's sweet voice didn't alter Gillian's mood.

"Not now. I want to take a nap."

"The guys want to barbecue for dinner and want us to join them. I'm making a potato salad and a chocolate cake."

Gillian remained silent.

"Can they use the barbecue?"

"I guess."

"You okay?" Gillian heard the concern in Samantha's voice.

Gillian placed the book on her tummy in frustration. "I'm fine. I just want to be alone."

"Okay."

Gillian tried to return to the book, but it was no use. She closed her eyes.

*****

17

Josh spent the afternoon on the beach with Samantha and Dusty. While the guys surfed, Samantha sunbathed in her hot pink bikini.

Josh snuck up and shook his wet hands all over her body.

Her eyes shot open. "Josh!"

He plopped down on his towel beside her. "The water's great. You should go in."

She ruffled Josh's wet hair. "Maybe later."

Dusty came up from the water's edge and lay down on the other side of Samantha. "Josh told me Gillian's a fourth grade teacher, but he didn't tell me what you do."

"I work for Social Services." Samantha brushed some sand off her beach towel. "I find deadbeat dads who haven't stepped up to the plate and supported their kids."

Dusty shielded his eyes from the sun. "So you're like a detective?"

"Sort of." She grabbed the tube of sunscreen.

"Sounds like a fun job."

"It is." Samantha eyed Dusty as she rubbed the pasty-white lotion onto her legs.

"Where's Gillian?" Josh asked.

"In her room." She rolled her eyes.

"On a beautiful day like this?" Josh shifted his legs and got sand on her towel. He brushed it off. "She'd feel better if she came outside."

"Yeah. Since her grandmother died, she's been kind of antisocial... and for some reason I feel like she's mad at me. I don't know why."

"I know she was upset because you didn't go to church today."

She rubbed some sunscreen on Josh's freckled shoulders and handed it to him. "I don't know why she's so upset about me not going to church." She handed the sunscreen to him. "She just isn't the same Gillian."

"How long has she had anorexia?" He tossed the sunscreen back to her and wiped the excess off on his towel.

"It probably started about a year ago." She leaned on her elbows, eyes surveying the horizon. "I first noticed it then. She was stressed out at school. She had a difficult class of students and her grandmother was sick."

"Have you talked to her about it?" Josh adjusted his sunglasses.

"No. She's in denial, so I figure I'd just be wasting my breath. Besides, I don't want her to get mad at me over it."

"Someone has to get through to her and I'll only be home on the weekends." Josh looked over at Dusty. "Dusty, will you talk to her?"

Dusty raised his head. "Me? Why me? Leave me out of this. I'm just the handyman, remember? She's your friend. Besides, I agree with

Samantha. I've heard unless a person acknowledges they have a problem, it's useless." Dusty picked up his surfboard and jogged into the water.

*****

Gillian stirred as Samantha's voice woke her.

"Gilly, you awake?"

"Yes."

"May I come in?" Samantha called from the doorway.

Gillian nodded as she sat up in bed and hugged her knees.

Samantha sat beside her. "What's the matter?"

"What do you mean?"

"Something's wrong. You're not yourself."

Gillian felt her brow furrow. "It bothers me you played hooky from church. Sometimes I feel like I'm the only responsible one around here."

Samantha put her hands on her hips. "You think I'm irresponsible?"

"Sam, I'm sorry."

"I find all those deadbeat dads..."

"Of course you do. I shouldn't have said what I did."

An uncomfortable silence fell on the room like when a condemned defendant is waiting for the jury to return with the verdict.

Gillian reached out and touched Samantha's hand. "Your parents asked about you at church."

"I know. They called." Samantha looked down at the carpet. "This is the first time in my life when I haven't had my parents telling me to go to church. I just decided not to go today. It doesn't mean I'm going to stop going all together." The ocean breeze puffed the white organdy curtains. Gillian's fingers traced the design of the afghan, remembering Gram, sitting by the fire, knitting.

Samantha squeezed her hand. "Are you going to tell me what happened between you and Josh last night?"

"It's nothing really. He thinks I'm too thin."

"Anything else?"

"You know I've always needed time to myself. I guess I'm feeling this way even more so since Gram died." Tears welled up in her eyes. Her finger ran around the edge of a yellow rose. "I miss Gram so much."

"I know." Samantha hugged her. "She was a great lady."

Gillian clung to Samantha, unable to let go.

Samantha sniffed the air. "I smell the barbecue. I think dinner will be ready soon."

Gillian wiped her tears away. "I'll be right down."

Chapter Five

Gillian scurried ahead of Samantha. "I'll get the door."

Samantha carried a hot casserole of baked beans toward the patio. Potato salad, steaming barbequed chicken, and cool drinks were already on the table. She placed the dish next to them on the table covered with a red and white checked tablecloth.

"Is there anything I can do?" Gillian smiled and felt more like a guest than the homeowner.

"Nope. Everything's done." Samantha took a seat next to Dusty.

Gillian sat at the empty place setting. She hoped Josh and Dusty wouldn't notice her red, swollen eyes.

Hungrier than she realized, Gillian ate with gusto. *I'll have to do extra sit-ups.* She looked up to see them watching her. "What?" She wiped barbeque sauce off her chin.

"Nothing," Samantha mumbled, taking a bite of potato salad.

Dusty licked the barbeque sauce off his fingers. "Tell me more about the camp you were talking about earlier."

"Royal Family Kids' Camps." Samantha turned toward him. "It's for abused and neglected children...foster kids. There are camps across the country sponsored by local churches, even some in other countries. Christians volunteer a week of their time as counselors, or the coach, activity director, or even a life guard. It takes a lot of volunteers to be a success."

Gillian sat up straighter. "The purpose of the camp is to give these kids a week of happy memories...memories they'll cherish."

Samantha smiled. "There's a dress-up center. Some little girls put on prom dresses over their swimsuits and walk around all day like princesses." She looked at Gillian. "Remember the little boy who wore the army uniform? He marched around with his shoulders back, chin up, looking so proud."

"Besides dressing up, they build things. Some paint or create crafts. We have tea parties for the girls...and, of course swimming. They love to swim." Gillian smiled at Josh for the first time since lunch.

"How much does it cost?" Dusty sipped his drink.

"It doesn't cost the children or their foster parents anything," Samantha said. "The money comes from donations."

"I'll bet it's hard to get donations." Dusty leaned his elbows on the table and clasped his hands together.

Gillian set her glass on the table. Dusty seems genuinely interested. "Not as hard as it is to get volunteers, especially male counselors for the boys."

Samantha added, "We've gotten money from individuals, some businesses, and a couple of grants. We still need to raise a couple of thousand for our camp this summer, I think." Samantha looked over at Gillian. "Am I right?"

Gillian nodded. "It's what I heard."

Josh wiped barbeque sauce off his fingers with a napkin. "I've heard the camp can change a kid's life."

"It's the best thing to ever happen to some of them. It gives them hope." Samantha added, "Not only kids'. It changes volunteers' lives too."

The setting sun left behind a horizon aflame in orange and yellow splashed across the darkened sky. "I'm going to go for a walk on the beach," Dusty said.

Samantha jumped up. "Mind if I tag along?"

Gillian watched Dusty and Samantha leave.

"Since everyone else made dinner, I guess it's only fair I clean up," Gillian stacked the dishes.

Josh stood. "I'll help." Once inside, Gillian handed Josh a dish towel. "I'll wash and you can dry."

"Dusty was really interested in Royal Family. Don't you think so?" She handed him a glass

Josh dried the tumbler and set it on the counter. Then leaned his backside against the counter and folded his arms across his chest. "Yeah, he did. Maybe you could talk him into volunteering...at the camp."

"Is he a Christian?"

"Don't know. Never asked."

"You know you have to be a Christian to be a part of Royal Family."

"I'll ask him."

Josh looked around the room. "It's like old times being in this kitchen with you. It looks just the same."

"I know." Gillian shrugged. "It needs a fresh look. The old wallpaper has got to go. I think I'm going to paint it a light yellow and put a border across the top." She pointed at the old wallpaper, trying to visualize it as she spoke. The water from her hands ran down her arms and made her giggle.

Josh smiled. "Have you ever removed wallpaper before?"

"No. Why?"

"It's messy. It can be a real pain getting the paper off. If you wait until the weekend, I can help."

"Thanks, but I want to get started on it tomorrow. If all goes well, I'll be finished by the end of the week. At least, I hope I will." Gillian pulled the plug for the water to drain out of the sink.

"I'm sure I'll be able to do something to help on weekends, even if it's holding boards for Dusty."

With the last dish dried, Josh was about to hang the dishtowel on the rack. Instead he snapped the towel on Gillian's backside.

Startled, she jumped. "Is this how it's going to be?" She grabbed a towel and readied it to snap at him, chasing him around the kitchen table and into the living room. Unable to reach him, she slumped onto the sofa, panting.

Josh crept toward her holding the towel above his head. "Truce?"

She laughed. "You're incorrigible."

"I've missed your laugh." He held the end of her towel and they sat silently until Samantha came through the door.

"How was the walk?" he asked.

"Glorious." Samantha plopped into the overstuffed chair, one leg dangled over the arm.

Josh yawned. "I guess I'll call it a night. I've got an early start tomorrow."

"Good night." Gillian followed him to the front door and locked it behind him.

After turning off the lights, Gillian and Samantha climbed the stairs.

*****

In the apartment, Dusty entered the bedroom wearing boxers. He toweled his hair, still wet from a shower. He lay down on his bed with his arms under his head and watched Josh.

"How was your walk on the beach with Sam?" Josh pulled a suitcase out of the closet and plopped it on the bed.

"It was okay."

"Just okay?"

"Yeah, why?" Dusty watched as Josh unzipped his suitcase.

"No reason. I just thought maybe something was happening between the two of you." Josh raised an eyebrow.

"Nah. She's cool, but she's not my type." Dusty turned on his side leaned on his elbow, and propped his head on his hand. "What about you and Gillian?"

"I got her to laugh tonight. I think it's the first time I've heard her laugh since we moved in."

"So you melted the Ice Queen, did you?" Dusty quipped. The edge in his voice surprised him.

"You're not being fair."

"As my Pop used to say, 'don't get your shorts in a wad.'"

Josh shot him a look.

It reminded Dusty of one of his teacher's expressions when he went too far. He held his hands in the air over his head. "Hey, man, all kidding aside. I apologize for calling her the Ice Queen. I know she's your friend. I shouldn't have said anything. Are we cool?"

"Yeah." Josh changed the subject. "So what do you plan to do tomorrow?"

"After catching some waves, I plan to start tearing out the stairs leading to the beach."

Josh zipped up his suitcase. "Do me a favor while I'm gone, would you?"

"It depends."

"Will you check in on Gillian? She plans to strip the kitchen wallpaper. From what I've heard, it can be a horrendous job. Maybe you could help her out?"

"I thought the deal was for me to do the outside work and she was going to do the painting on the inside." *It isn't like I don't want to help. I'm not keen on being with her in the face of a massive project.* He pictured the tiny, edgy woman in a volcano of pasty paper and he shuddered at the thought.

"It would just be nice to check in on her. Is it too much to ask?" Josh left the room, rolling his suitcase behind him.

Dusty called after him. "Okay, only for you."

When sleep evaded Dusty, he crept from the bedroom, careful not to wake Josh. After pacing the living room floor, he sat on the sofa and rested his head against the back cushion. *Pop... I miss you.* He wiped warm tears away with his rough hands. For three years, he'd locked his feelings in a vault. No one could imagine the grief he felt for the man who meant everything to him. His emotions, dormant for so long, awakened.

Chapter Six

Gillian hugged the American flag close to her chest as she tramped through the damp grass, past the weed infested rose garden, to the edge of the cliff. She raised the flag just as she had done every morning since her grandmother died. It felt so good to pump her arms and watch the flag unfurl and flap in the ocean breeze. She paused and peered over the cliff. Below, Dusty sat on his surfboard in the calm water, waiting for the perfect wave. He bobbed serenely with the lull of the ocean. *His surfboard must mean as much to him as my piano does to me.* She sighed, then whispered a short prayer, "Dear Lord, help me be a witness for You."

Entering the house, Gillian brewed a cup of Earl Grey, grabbed her Bible and favorite devotional, and curled up in the familiar overstuffed floral chair. Quiet time with her Creator was, in her mind, the only way to start the day. *I need God's power the way Dusty needs a powerful wave.*

Later, she made her bed, washed the few dishes in the kitchen sink, put a load of laundry in the washer, and sat at the table in the kitchenette. She started a list of things she needed to paint the inside of the house. She jotted down, "brushes, paint, roller". She wrote a note in the margin, "have Dusty bring the big heavy ladder in from the garage."

She eyed the old wallpaper of peppermills on a tan background. It had to be at least thirty years old. *It's gotta go.* She tapped the pen against her cheek then made another note in the margin, "check out wallpaper borders". *I'll check out wallpaper borders today.*

She left her list on the table and went upstairs to freshen up. Clad in a pair of white shorts and a red tank top, she washed her face, applied some lip gloss, and redid her pony tail. As she looked in the mirror, she wondered what Josh saw when he looked at her. The pounding of a hammer drifted through the open window. *Aha, my handyman has emerged from the sea.* She slipped on some sandals, grabbed her purse, and the list from the kitchen table.

Curious, she went to the edge of the cliff and looked down. Below, Dusty pried the rotten boards apart and tossed them to the side of the incline. She called, "I thought you were just going to replace the worst ones."

He leaned his elbow on his knee, and looked up. "The whole thing is in bad shape, and it's dangerous." He squinted against the sun and wiped the sweat off his forehead with his arm.

"I guess you know best." She shrugged. "I'm going to Home Depot to pick up some things." She turned to leave.

"Wait up." He climbed the rickety old stairs two at a time and when she turned around he had reached the top and was face to face with her. His tan body glistened with sweat. "I need to order some lumber, nails, and things. How about I go with you?"

She hesitated. "I was going to do some other errands too. I need to go to the market."

"Me too. I don't have a thing in my refrigerator," he said, with a feminine flip of his wrist.

She smiled with a hint of a smirk. "Okay."

"I'll drive. I have more room in my car."

*****

While Dusty headed for the lumber section at Home Depot, Gillian stopped at the paint department. She picked several shades of yellow. Her favorite looked like the color of a lemon chiffon pie -- light and cheerful, just what she was looking for.

I'll leave the wallpaper with the tiny dusty rose flowers in my bedroom, but what about the living room? I'm going to concentrate on the kitchen. It's a big enough project for now. She sighed.

Dusty came up behind her. "The lumber for the stairs is ordered and it'll be delivered tomorrow."

She turned to face him. "Don't I need to pay for it?"

"I did. You can reimburse me." He handed her the receipt.

She looked at the amount, her brows knitted in confusion. *He has this much cash with him?*

She realized he was staring at her. "I don't know how much paint I need for the kitchen."

"A gallon should be plenty." He eyed the paint can. "I like the color."

"I need a can of white paint for the cupboards, and I want to pick out new hardware for them too." Her mind whirled. "Do you know where the wallpaper is?"

"No. I'll find a clerk to help us." He headed down the aisle to look for a salesperson while Gillian followed him with her eyes. *He sure is a take charge kind of guy. I'm not sure if I like it or not.*

Soon Dusty returned with his arms loaded. He tumbled the items into the shopping cart. He held up a strange looking tool. "The Wall Claw makes holes in the wallpaper. It's supposed to help remove wallpaper easier." He dropped it into the cart.

"I guess I'll find out." She filled the shopping cart with masking tape, brushes, rollers, and the paint, crossing off each item on her list.

"I think I've got everything I need. I'll wait to pick out the border for another time."

Leaving the parking lot, Dusty said, "I'm starved. How about some lunch?"

"Okay."

"McDonalds?"

"Sure." Soon they sat at a table inside McDonalds, their order stacked on a tray in the center of the table. Dusty divided up the food. "I think I may have some good news for you."

"What good news?"

"I checked under the house today. The foundation, wiring, and plumbing all look in good shape. Whoever built the house did a good job. It's solid." He chomped his burger.

"It's more than good news. It's great news." She sighed and said a silent prayer, thanking God. "I wondered what the noise was under the house this morning." She moved her salad around with a plastic fork, and sipped her iced tea.

"You seem distracted."

"Sorry." It's just...I've never removed wallpaper...and I've heard it can be quite a chore."

"I'll do whatever I can."

"Would you bring the ladder inside and move the refrigerator and stove away from the wall for me?"

"You bet."

*****

"I'm home," Samantha called, as she came through the kitchen door. She stopped suddenly. "Wow!"

"Are you sure you don't mean 'ugh' instead?" Gillian held up a glob of old wallpaper in her rubber gloved hand.

Dusty glanced in Samantha's direction while he continued to work. "Hi."

Samantha stood with her hands on her hips. "What a mess!"

"You can help, if you want." Gillian brushed her hair off her forehead with her arm.

"Well..." Samantha looked at Dusty. "Sure. I'll just change into some grubbies first." She sashayed through the kitchen.

"If you're thinking about dinner, the kitchen's closed," Gillian said.

"I'll order pizza," Samantha called, heading to change her clothes.

They worked tirelessly stripping the walls. Dusty stood on the ladder while Gillian worked below him. A glob of wet wallpaper fell on her head.

"Hey." She tried to pull the stuff out of her hair, and only made more of a mess with her gooey gloved hands. She pitched the glob toward Dusty, but he ducked just in time.

He jumped down from the ladder, grabbed more ammunition, and threw it at Gillian. Samantha joined them. "Let's get him."

Dusty was quick and missed most of what was thrown his way, but with two against one he got his share.

"Ceasefire!" Dusty held up his hands from behind a cabinet door.

Later they sat on the floor, gunk dripping from head to toe, laughing and eating pizza. Gillian picked the pepperoni and sausage off her slice and put it on a napkin.

Samantha sipped her Pepsi. "Dusty do you remember last night when I talked about Royal Family Kid's Camps. I'm passionate about it. You can probably tell by my enthusiasm." Samantha took another sip of her drink. "What are you passionate about, Dusty?"

"Removing wallpaper." He smirked.

Gillian looked up to see his grin.

"Nah." He shrugged. "Surfing, I guess."

"Well, it's a given," Samantha said. "Anything else?"

"I'll have to think about it."

"What about you, Gillian?" he asked.

"Me?"

"Yeah."

"I have my students, my music... but for now, all I want to do is finish the kitchen," Gillian said, followed by a laugh.

Samantha and Dusty laughed with her.

Gillian wiped her mouth with a napkin. "I've had it. Let's call it a night."

Dusty stood. "I'll help you clean up this mess in the morning."

After Dusty left and Samantha had gone to bed, Gillian reclined in a hot bubble bath, trying to relieve her sore shoulders and back. She remembered him saying he'd help her clean up the mess in the morning, and she felt confident he would. *Maybe he's more than a surfer. Only time would tell.* Although she was exhausted, she grinned at her sense of accomplishment with the kitchen prepared and ready for paint. She closed her eyes and scooted down deeper into the warm bath water and remembered the day -- the way he whistled as he worked, shopping and working together. Today she had discovered a gentle side to him, and she liked it.

There would always be Gram, like the strong foundation of the house. She had her memories of her and no one could ever take them away from her. Yet she knew she could not live in the past. Today she had made a fresh start -- a new beginning. *I look forward to what tomorrow will bring.*

Chapter Seven

The next morning Gillian awoke early, ready to tackle the kitchen. First she would do what she always did. She cradled the flag and tromped through the dew covered lawn, past the rose garden to the flagpole. After she raised it, she walked to the edge of the cliff and peered down at the water.

Behind her, Dusty asked, "How's the surf?"

Gillian jumped and turned to face him. "You startled me." Heat rose to her cheeks as she clutched her chest.

"Sorry. I didn't mean to scare you." He smiled.

She shaded her eyes with her hand. "The water looks nice."

"Do you surf?"

"I bodysurf."

He held a surfboard at his side. His hair looked like it hadn't been combed, but it didn't matter next to his chiseled jaw and dreamy hazel eyes.

She cleared her throat. "I've got lots to do today, so I'd better get started."

"I'll come with you."

"Aren't you going surfing?"

"I'll go later." He looked at her quizzically. "I waited 'til you got up. I promised to help clean up the mess we made last night."

"I usually spend time doing my devotions first thing in the morning." She paused. "I guess I can do them later."

He propped his surfboard against the garage and they entered the house and started tidying up. "Do you mean like meditation?"

"Not in the Eastern sense. I don't chant. I read an inspirational story from a devotional book, then I read my Bible, and... I write my prayers in a journal."

Dusty scooped up old wallpaper and stuffed it into a trash bag.

Was he mulling over what she'd said? She had to know. "Are you a Christian?"

"Yeah." He stopped what he was doing and looked at her with a surprised look. "Of course. I appreciate God's creation... and I'm a good person."

"Do you have a personal relationship with Jesus?"

Before he could answer, they were interrupted by a knock at the door.

Gillian opened the door. A Home Depot delivery man stood on the front stoop, a clipboard in his hand.

Dusty skirted around Gillian. "I'll show you where to unload it."

She expected Dusty to return after the delivery truck left, but he didn't. *I had the perfect opportunity to invite him to church. Why didn't I? I won't let another day go by without inviting him.* No more missed opportunities she vowed. As she painted, she heard pounding and boards splitting in the distance. *He's working on tearing out the old stairs.*

After dinner and a shower, Gillian sat in the overstuffed chair in the living room reading her Bible. She heard laughter and peered out the window to see who was there. Samantha and Dusty held hands as they promenaded toward the cliff. Samantha carried a six pack of beer.

Gillian felt betrayed as jealousy washed over her. *I want him to hold my hand and laugh with me.* A knot twisted in her stomach. *Why should I care? But I do.*

Chapter Eight

The next morning, Gillian and Samantha sat across from each other at the table in the kitchenette. The silence shattered with spoons tapping cups, coffee slurped, and waves crashing rhythmically in the distance. Gillian avoided Samantha's eyes like a stranger on a bus.

Samantha cleared her throat. "How long are you going to give me the silent treatment?"

"I'm reading the paper."

"Since when do you read the newspaper without even speaking to me?"

Gillian laid the *Orange County Register* on the table. "I don't know who you are anymore."

"What do you mean?"

Gillian finally looked in her eyes. "You've acted different, especially since Dusty came."

"It's the beer, isn't it? You're judging me for having a beer?"

"Some alcoholics started with only one beer!"

"Gillian, I'm not your mom."

Gillian sipped her tea. "It isn't just... you don't act like yourself when he's around."

"He makes me laugh."

"Obviously." Gillian held the newspaper in front of her face. She blocked her view of Samantha and tried to read, but couldn't concentrate on any of the articles.

Samantha sighed. "I've got to get ready for work. I like Dusty. Is he going to come between us?"

Gillian remained mute, hidden behind the newspaper.

Samantha stood. "I'm having dinner with some people from work tonight. So I won't be home 'til late."

After Samantha left, Gillian put down the newspaper. *Why? Why? Why am I such a self-righteous egotist?* Sometimes she hated herself for how she acted. Sometimes her actions had a mind of their own. She prayed, "Dear Lord, please forgive me for my sin of self-righteousness. Help me change, I pray." She felt God's forgiveness, yet she knew she needed to change.

Later, Gillian took her Bible and teacher's guide and sat on a chaise lounge on the patio with a tablet. She wrote notes and a list of supplies to use as visuals for her Sunday school class. The Bible story was about David and Jonathan's friendship. How appropriate.

After she prepared Sunday's lesson, she felt a sense of accomplishment and went inside to stow her things. Then she placed her fingers on the smooth keys of the baby grand and practiced the offertory she'd play during Sunday's worship service, "Come, Thou Fount." She sang as she played the old familiar hymn.

Come, Thou Fount of ev'ry blessing;
Tune my heart to sing Thy grace.
Streams of mercy, never ceasing,
Call for songs of loudest praise.
Teach me some melodious sonnet
Sung by flaming tongues above;
Praise the mount -- I'm fixed upon it --

She practiced the piece over and over. She took time with each measure, exacting the perfect tempo; she closed her eyes and touched the keys gently, creating a whispered, wordless prayer of her redeemer's love. At sunset, Gillian took the flag down and carefully folded it. On her way back to the house, Dusty came up from the beach and stood at the top of the new stairs.

"I plan to start the prep work on the outside of the house tomorrow. Have you decided on a color?" he asked.

"The same as it's always been. I think it's called cobalt blue."

"Should I get it?"

He stood in front of her, his surfboard at his side. Distracted by his tan, wet, and sandy body, she felt a strange pang, something she'd never felt before. "What?"

"I asked you if you'd like me to get the paint... for the house?"

"Yes... Sure... just bring me the receipt. So I can reimburse you." She walked away.

He called after her, "I heard you play the piano today."

She turned and looked at him.

"You're good."

"Thanks." She clutched the flag to her chest and her face redden.

Later that night, Gillian waited for Samantha in the living room, an unread novel in her lap. She'd rehearsed her apology all day. When Samantha came through the door Gillian jumped up. "I'm sorry...about what I said this morning. Will you forgive me?"

"Of course." Samantha put her purse on a table by the door. "I'm sorry too. I think you may be right about how I act when I'm around Dusty." She sat on the sofa and kicked off her shoes. "I think we just had our first argument."

"You're right." Gillian shut the book. "I hope it's the only one."

Chapter Nine

Dusty stirred in the twin bed and looked over at Josh. "What time is it?"

Josh picked up the clock on the bedside table, and stared at it. "I can't believe it. It's ten o'clock."

Dusty jumped out of bed and headed toward the bathroom.

Josh sat on the edge of the bed and ran his hand through his bed hair. "What's for breakfast?"

"Nothing," Dusty called from the bathroom.

"Why don't we go out?"

"Sounds good to me. Give me five minutes." Dusty turned on the shower.

Josh grabbed a newspaper from the rack as they entered the restaurant. An older waitress brought coffee and took their order. "What part do you want?" Josh held up the newspaper.

"I'll take the business section."

Josh shot Dusty a curious look. "Is there a side of you I don't know about?"

Dusty didn't respond.

Before their order arrived, Josh straightened. "Listen to this." He read aloud the community news ad, "Adult Children of Alcoholics meets at the Oasis Senior Center on Wednesday nights at seven."

The waitress shuffled to the table loaded down with their order. Josh held the paper to one side so the waitress could put the warm plates of bacon, eggs, and pancakes in front of them.

"More coffee?" she asked.

"Yes, please," Josh said.

Dusty held up his cup for her to refill.

Josh folded the newspaper and put it in the seat next to him. "You've got to get Gillian to go." He salt and peppered his eggs.

"I don't know. She isn't the least bit interested. And I don't even know where it is," Dusty said. He spread strawberry jelly on his wheat toast.

"It isn't far." He poured maple syrup on his pancakes.

"I'll see."

"If you'll agree to take her, I'll get her to go with you," Josh said. "What do you say?"

"If it's the only way I'm going to get you off my back."

Josh grinned.

Dusty changed the subject. "So, how was your week on the road?"

"There's a lot to learn...and I know I don't want to be a salesman for the rest of my life." Josh dabbed a piece of pancake into the runny egg yolk. "I plan to send my resume to other places." He plunged the gooey bite into his mouth. "What about you... and those great stairs you built."

Dusty smiled.

"I couldn't believe it when I got home last night and you had finished them. I told you I'd help."

"Well, you know our landlord. She's a hard taskmaster."

Dusty wadded up his napkin and tossed it in his empty plate. "You'll have to see the kitchen."

"You did it too?"

"I only helped get rid of the old wallpaper. Gillian did most of the work."

"Were you able to surf?" Josh pushed his plate away.

"Yeah, I did." Dusty pulled out his wallet and picked up the check. "I'll get breakfast."

*****

Gillian sat in the big overstuffed chair with her Bible, teacher's guide, a tablet, and a pen in her lap. Deep in thought, she jotted notes of things she wanted to remember to do for her class.

Samantha ambled down the stairs, her hair in snarls -- looked like something had nested in it. She yawned. "What time is it anyway?"

Gillian glanced at her watch. "Noon."

"You're kidding?"

"Would I kid you?"

Gillian watched as Samantha went to the refrigerator and stood with the door open. Samantha opened the hydrator and pulled out a plum, rubbed it on her pajamas, and took a bite. As juice ran down her chin, she grabbed a napkin and wiped it off. She wandered back into the living room and plopped down on the sofa. "I'm going shopping. Wanna come along?"

Gillian didn't look up from her lesson. "No thanks."

"Come on Gilly. It'll be fun."

"No. I really want to make some things for my class tomorrow and I have everything I need to make them."

"You can do it later."

"I don't want to wait 'til later. I want to do it now. Besides, I'm not ready and I don't have any money to shop." Gillian continued to make notes.

34

"You could window shop." Samantha wrapped the napkin around the plum pit and held it in her lap. "You know I don't like to shop alone."

"Call one of your friends from work. "

Samantha was silent.

"Josh stopped by a little while ago and asked me to go out tonight," Gillian said nonchalantly.

"He did?"

"Yeah."

"Just you two?"

"I think so."

"Where're you going?" Samantha sat on the edge of the sofa.

"I don't know."

Samantha got up, threw her plum pit in the trash under the kitchen sink, and returned to the living room. "Come on Gilly... p-l-e-a-s-e... go shopping with me." She got down on her knees in front of Gillian, with her hands folded like in prayer. "I'll even help you with your lesson."

Gillian softened. "You're ridiculous. Get up off your knees." She sighed. "I'll go with you on one condition."

Samantha jumped up. "What? Anything."

"You can make up some Jeopardy-type questions on Queen Esther. The kids like to play games." Gillian looked at Samantha "You remember the story of Queen Esther, don't you?"

"Of course." Samantha's brow furrowed. "I went to Sunday school too. Remember?"

"Yes. I do." Gillian smiled as she handed her Bible to Samantha, opened at the book of Esther. "Here. You can write the questions on these three-by-five cards." Gillian raced up the stairs. "I'm going to gather up some bathrobes and stuff, and make a crown out of poster board and glitter. They love to perform the Bible stories."

Gillian came down the stairs loaded with bathrobes, sashes, sheets, and jewelry. She dumped them onto the sofa. "Look at this." She held up a sheer panel, probably once a curtain. "Won't it be great for Queen Esther?"

"Yeah. Great." Samantha sat with a pen poised above a blank index card. She gazed into space.

"On second thought, I'll write the questions." Gillian dashed to the den and soon emerged with a large sheet of yellow poster board, scissors, glue, a ruler, and a container of glitter. "You can do the crown."

"You're such a controller."

"I am not." Gillian laid all the supplies on the table in front of Samantha. "It's called leadership. And someone has to do it." Gillian smiled.

"This crown will be a masterpiece. Even the queen of England will want to wear it." Samantha chewed her lower lip as she sketched.

*****

Josh paddled out to where Dusty sat on his surfboard waiting for a wave. He maneuvered his board to be next to Dusty. "I've got a date with Gillian tonight!"

They caught a wave and rode it into shore, then paddled back out to catch another one. As they waited, Dusty asked, "So where are you going to take her?"

"I've made dinner reservations at White Horses in San Clemente." *Should I tell him I plan to ask Gillian to marry me?* Josh shook off the thought. *No, Gillian needs to be the first one to hear my proposal, not Dusty.*

They surfed all afternoon until four o'clock, when Josh headed for the apartment to shave and shower. Josh rehearsed what he wanted to say to Gillian, soapy water running down his body. "Gilly, I've never found anyone I've cared more about than you. I love you, and I think you love me too." *No, it's too soon. Or is it? I want her to know how I feel.* He tried another approach, "Gillian, I've loved you since the third grade, will you marry me?" *No. No. No. It's all wrong.*

He tried again. "You know I've always loved you. Let's make it legal!" *Sounds sappy.* He stepped out of the shower and dried off. *What if she say's no? I couldn't handle it.*

During the week he had planned the romantic evening. After dinner, he'd drive to a secluded spot and propose.

Maybe it's too soon after her grandmother's death, and she's almost obsessed with the restoration of the house. It'll be a while before I'll be able to offer her financial support with school loans looming over me...just starting my new job -- and a traveling job to boot. Maybe I should wait until I have more to offer. He wiped the steam off the mirror, like it would remove all his doubts.

*****

When Samantha and Gillian arrived home from their shopping trip, Gillian climbed out of her VW and headed for the house while Samantha lingered beside the car, holding a number of shopping bags.

Samantha watched as Dusty appeared at the top of the stairs, coming up from the beach with a surfboard under his arm. *What a hunk he is. Be still my beating heart.*

He shook his wet, sandy mane. "It looks like you bought out the store."

36

"Not quite." Samantha looked down coyly. "Josh and Gillian are going out tonight. You want to grab a bite to eat with me?"

Dusty raked his hand through his matted hair without much success. "I make great spaghetti. How about I fix you dinner?"

"Sounds w-o-n-d-e-r-f-u-l."

"Give me about an hour to shower and straighten the place, then come up."

She squinted against the bright sun. "Can I bring something?"

"Just yourself."

She watched him trudge across the lawn toward his apartment and bit her lip, trying to stifle a jubilant scream.

Samantha raced to the house, her heart pounding out of her chest. She realized the beat didn't come from exertion, but from excitement. As she dumped out the bags on her bed, she sorted through what she planned to wear. After clipping off the price tags, she stepped into a pair of white shorts and pulled one of the new tops she had bought over her head. She combed her hair and flipped it behind her ears. Gold jewelry and new sandals completed her outfit. She gazed at her reflection in the mirror and admired the lime green scooped neckline top, which showed some cleavage. She heard a tap at her bedroom door.

Gillian entered and twirled. "How do I look?"

"Fabulous."

"Trying on your new clothes?"

"Yep."

Gillian looked her up and down. "You've always had a flair for fashion." She smiled. "Well, I'm off."

"See ya later."

Samantha left and soon tapped on the door of the apartment.

"Come in."

Dusty stood at the kitchen sink. A dishtowel tied around his waist covered his cutoffs. She clutched her top at the sight of him. *Stop my pounding heart.*

She strolled over to where he stood. "Can I help?"

"You can grab the wine glasses out of the cabinet above you." Using a corkscrew, he expertly slid the cork from the mouth of the wine bottle, poured the wine, and handed a glass to her. "Here's to... friendship."

They clicked their glasses. She had hoped for more than friendship and tried to hold his gaze, but he put his glass down and stirred the bubbling sauce.

Holding her wine glass, she moseyed around the sparsely furnished one room combination kitchen and living room. She picked up a photo on the end table and examined it more closely. "Who's this?"

"My mother."

"She's beautiful."

"Yep." He opened the oven door and slid the garlic bread into the gaping cavity.

She watched him. *He's putting Wolfgang Puck to shame.*

"Want to toss the salad?" Without waiting for an answer he added, "The dressing is next to the salad in the refrigerator."

She mixed the salad as he plopped the garlic bread into a red-and-white-checked napkin-lined bread basket and covered it to keep it warm. She put the Koa wood serving bowl and the matching salad bowls on the table. While the wine glasses and the salad bowls were nice, the plates and silverware looked like they came from a second hand store.

"Sorry for the lack of ambiance," he said as he brought the plates of spaghetti to the table. He held out the chair for her and he sat at the head of the table next to her.

"The music's nice. I didn't think you'd be a classical kind of guy."

"Will wonders never cease?" He handed her the salad bowl and after helping herself she passed it back to him, and took a bite of spaghetti.

"Umm. This is fantastic! Is there anything you can't do?" It sounded more like a statement instead of a question.

"Lots of things, I'm sure."

"Do you have a photo of your dad too?"

"Yeah." He wiped his mouth with a napkin and sipped his wine. "Since he died before I was born, I don't have many pictures of him."

"I'm sorry."

"I can't complain. I had a good childhood, nothing like the kids you work with."

"What about brothers and sisters?"

"Nope."

"Have you ever spent any time around kids?"

"Not really." He looked at her quizzically. "Why? Are you thinking of recruiting me for your camp?"

"I'm always thinking about it."

"Did they get the rest of the money they needed for the camp?"

"Yeah. In fact, someone anonymously donated ten thousand dollars!"

He grinned. "Great. More wine?"

"Maybe just a little." She held her glass as he poured.

He pushed himself away from the table.

She helped him clear and stacked the dishes on the counter. "I'll wash the dishes."

"Leave 'em. The maid will do them in the morning." He stretched. "You like Seinfeld?"

"I love it."

He strolled over to the DVD player and inserted the disk, then joined her on the sofa.

*****

Josh held the door open as Gillian slipped into the passenger seat, then he moved around to the driver's side and sat behind the steering wheel.

"I think Dusty and Samantha are getting together tonight."

"Dusty invited her up for spaghetti." Josh started the car.

"Samantha is gaga over him."

"She's pretty obvious, isn't she?" He backed out of the driveway.

"I thought maybe I was the only one who noticed."

"Samantha's always been a flirt, but we love her anyway."

"I guess I expected her to mature a little by now." Gillian looked over at him. "Do you think Dusty's interested in her?"

"He says he isn't. Who knows? He did invite her to dinner."

Arriving at the restaurant, Josh parked the car and, placing his hand on the small of her back, they strolled along the San Clemente Pier, arriving at the White Horses Restaurant & Bar with the white linen tablecloths and napkins, and a single rose on each table. Local art adorned the walls.

After being seated, they perused the menus. "What sounds good to you?" Josh asked.

"I can't decide between the chicken and the halibut. And the Mahi-Mahi is marinated in rum and vanilla and served with black beans and rice. Um... it all sounds so yummy." Her eyes went from one item to the other, trying to decide. "How about you?"

"It's either the salmon or the Filet Mignon with garlic and parsley butter. I think the Filet Mignon is going to win out though." He put down the menu.

"I'll have the Mahi-Mahi."

When the waiter arrived to take their order, Josh said, "She'll have the Mahi-Mahi and I'll have the Filet Mignon."

Gillian glanced around the room at the art displayed. "This is really nice."

"Not at all like Ruby's."

"I don't go out to nice places like this."

"You deserve it!"

Their salads arrived and Gillian unfolded her napkin and laid it in her lap, smoothing it across her legs. With her fork she poked around in the salad, like she was looking for something. "How's the job going?"

"Better than I expected. I work on commission and my sales were great last week."

"Good for you. I'm not surprised. When we had a fundraiser at school, you were always the one to sell the most candy bars. Or when our youth group had a food drive for the King's Cupboard, you always showed all of us up with the most cans collected. Joshy, you're turning red!"

She used the name his mother called him when he was a boy.

"It must be from surfing today."

When their order arrived, Gillian moved her salad to one side.

Josh noticed she ate her fish, but left the beans and rice. *Everything's going as planned. Later we'll stroll on the beach in the moonlight. It's then I'll ask her to marry me.*

Finished with his meal, Josh placed his fork and knife across the top of his plate, leaned back in the chair, and gazed at her. "I read in the paper today about a recovery group meeting at the Senior Center."

Gillian glared at him.

"Please... will you go to at least one meeting... for me?" He reached across the table and touched her hand. "Dusty said he'd take you."

"Why would he?"

"Maybe because he's my friend and he's doing it for me. Or maybe he's concerned about you too."

"So you and Dusty have been talking about me?"

"We all want what's best for you...Samantha too."

"So you've all been talking about me behind my back?"

"It's only because we care about you."

"I can't believe you've all ganged up against me."

"You've got it all wrong."

"Excuse me." She stood, threw her napkin on the table, and dashed to the ladies lounge. In her haste she almost knocked into a busboy in the aisle.

Josh sat alone at the table for two. He checked his watch. He sipped his water. He checked his watch again. He averted the stares. How long will she be?

When Gillian returned, she stood across the table from him. "Please take me home." Her eyes were red from the tears she'd shed.

"Gilly..." He reached for her hand.

"Now."

He shrugged. "Okay."

Unlike the evening he had planned of strolling along the beach in the moonlight, they rode back to Reagan Beach in silence.

After he pulled the car into the driveway and parked, Gillian raced to the house. With shoulders slumped, Josh trudged up the stairs to the apartment. Dusty and Samantha sat on the couch sipping wine when Josh opened the door. Dusty's head rested on the back of the sofa, his feet propped up on the coffee table.

"How was your date?" Samantha asked, her legs tucked under her.

"A disaster." Josh pulled up a kitchen chair and sitting on it backwards he joined them. He rested his arms on the back of the chair and put his chin on them. "Gilly thinks we've been talking about her behind her back."

"We have," Dusty said.

"It's only because we care about her," Josh said.

"Still, we shouldn't be talking about her behind her back." Dusty sat up straighter on the sofa and stretched from side to side.

"Then what do we do?" Samantha asked.

It was quiet while they thought, except for the drone of dialogue coming from the TV.

"What about an intervention?" Josh asked.

Samantha set her wine glass down on the coffee table. "It seems like a last resort...and I'm not willing to take the chance of losing her friendship over it. Besides, it wasn't so long ago she lost her grandmother." She tucked her blonde hair behind her ear. "You can count me out."

Josh looked at Dusty. "I don't suppose you'd be interested?"

"Like I said before, unless she realizes she has a problem she isn't going to get better."

Without the support of his friends, Josh felt like he was in a riptide, and knowing riptides, he knew he had to wait it out. "I'm going to bed. See you guys in the morning."

"Night, Josh," Samantha said.

"Night," Dusty echoed.

*****

Sleep evaded Gillian, as thoughts flashed through her mind like shooting stars. She thought about counting sheep. She even thought about getting up and reading a book, but she knew she wouldn't be able to concentrate on a plot with her mind on something other than the story. Finally she succumbed to prayer. "Father, why do I wait so long to come to you when I'm in trouble? Is it me, Lord? Am I wrong? Do I have an eating disorder? I don't think I do. Maybe they're right. Help me, I pray. And Lord, please help me get some sleep. Amen."

She was still tossing and turning when she heard Samantha close the front door and climb the stairs. Glancing at the clock's illuminated dial on the bedside table, she groaned. It was one o'clock in the morning.

Gillian heard Samantha stop outside her bedroom door. *Please don't knock. I don't want to talk.* She listened as Samantha tiptoed down the hall. Gillian sighed with relief.

Chapter Ten

The warmth of the afternoon sun penetrated Gillian's back as she knelt in the rose garden. Careful not to be scratched by thorns, she poked the screwdriver into the moist soil she'd watered the night before and pulled another weed and dropped it into the cardboard box at her side.

Dusty approached and stood over her. "We've been working all morning. How about a break?"

"I've got too much to do."

"I'll make you a deal. If you take a break with me now, I'll help you attack the weeds later?"

"Are you sure?"

"I'm sure." He reached for her hand.

Gillian felt like the jury was still out about Dusty. Sometimes she liked him, like when he helped strip the wallpaper, and other times she wasn't sure. She couldn't put her finger on anything in particular. *Maybe I'm paranoid.* His grin did the same thing to her just like her student Marcus' grin did. Marcus knew how to get his way with her and it was like Dusty did too. And Josh and Samantha liked him. She decided to give him a chance. "What do you have in mind?"

"How about a surfing lesson?"

She sat on her haunches and pulled off her gardening gloves, then stood. "You're on. I'll be down in a few minutes."

Gillian raced upstairs and yanked open the bottom dresser drawer. *I know it's in here somewhere.* She kept digging, looking for her favorite black one-piece swimsuit. After she rummaged around through layers of shorts and T-shirts, she pulled it out.

She slid into the sleek suit. *Dusty must be growing on me. He's not the same guy I met the first day. I like his smile and his sense of humor.*

While she peered at herself in the full length mirror, she noticed the suit didn't fit as it once did. She grabbed the extra fabric in her hands. *Could they be right? Do I have a problem? Nah.* She buried the thought as she slipped on a sheer cover-up, redid her ponytail, and slipped into some flip-flops.

As she clomped down the new stairs to the beach below, she spotted Dusty on his surfboard, in the water. She laid her beach towel next to his, dropped her cover-up, and strolled to the water's edge. Dusty rode a wave toward shore to meet her as she waded into the water.

With Gillian on top of his board, he towed her out beyond the breakers. "It's a lot like body surfing as far as how to catch a wave." He put the leash around her ankle.

"What are you doing?" she gasped.

"It's for when you go one way and the board goes the other."

"What makes you think I'll fall off?"

"The ocean is powerful. Trust me."

"I feel like a dog."

He smiled. "Believe me, you don't look like one." Dusty held onto the edge of the board and stayed beside her in the water as she chose a wave and waited for it. As it neared, she paddled furiously toward shore. She caught it just right and felt it lift and carry her. She guided the board like she had on many rubber raft rides. Dusty bodysurfed beside her. With the ride over, they turned and waded out into deeper water again.

"It's easy," she said. Droplets from her wet pony tail trickled down her back.

"Oh it was, was it?" He laughed. "You haven't stood up on the board yet."

*****

Gillian and Dusty trudged up to their towels and plopped down. The warm sun dried her body.

Dusty turned on his side and faced her. "I think it's a nice thing you do... raising the flag every day."

"I do it in honor my grandmother." She felt the tears puddle in her eyes. "It was her tradition...she meant everything to me."

Dusty reached over and wiped the tear from her cheek. "How long did your grandmother live here?"

"Since she was a bride. My grandfather had the house built for her. He was in the Navy and when he was out to sea, she prayed God would protect him. She said the ocean somehow became a promise, you know, like the rainbow was to Noah."

Gillian watched as Dusty's brows knitted. She forgot he might not know the biblical story of Noah. "The rainbow was a sign from God he'd never destroy the earth with a flood again."

"Oh."

"Anyway, when Grandpa came back safely, by sea, of course, Gram decided she'd never leave the coast again."

"I wish I'd met her. I'd teach her how to surf."

"Actually, Gram bodysurfed every day. She taught me. And she loved to watch the surfers from the cliff."

"It seems to be another tradition you've carried on. I saw you check me out the other day." He smiled his full, toothy grin and then evaded her elbow like a running back.

After a brief silence, Gillian said, "Gram was always there for me. She taught me how to play the piano...and gave me the love of books...and children. Thank God I got her genes and not my parents'. She loved God with all her heart. She wasn't a Bible thumping Christian, but she started every day on her knees. She prayed for me and for so many others. She was my model and I want to be just like her."

Dusty let sand run through his fingers. "I... I... had someone who meant a lot to me too," he said, still looking down. "It was my grandfather." He looked up and caught and held Gillian's gaze. "He died a couple of years ago, and I haven't talked about him to anyone except my mother. She's the only one who understands what he meant to me."

"I know what you mean. I don't think anyone understands the relationship I had with my grandmother either. Not even Sam." Dusty appeared to be more sensitive than she realized in the beginning. Now when she looked into his eyes, she saw a depth of compassion.

"My grandfather didn't talk about God, but I know he believed in God. I could tell by how he loved nature and how he appreciated God's creation. He's the one who taught me how to surf. He always encouraged me to be my own person and gave me more opportunities than most people ever get. He took me to everything from professional ball games to the San Francisco Opera."

Gillian lay on her stomach, her head rested on her crossed arms as she looked at Dusty beside her on his towel. She listened with interest.

"Pop was bald and stocky, but in my eyes he was a giant with keen blue eyes, and he gave me every advantage I could have dreamed."

He brushed away a tear. "This is the first time I've talked about him since he died."

"He sounds like someone I'd liked to have known."

Later Dusty sat up. "I'm famished. How about I pick up some Chinese for dinner?"

"Sounds good. Sam will be home soon."

"I'll get enough for the three of us." He stood and reached down to help her up. She grasped his hand and he pulled her up so quickly she was caught off balance and fell into him. Being so close to him and holding his hand, she felt the chemistry between them. It was intoxicating.

*****

45

Gillian took a shower and applied a little make-up. She put on a clean pair of navy blue shorts and a white knit T-shirt. Later Samantha burst through the door followed by Dusty, carrying two bags of food.

They gathered around the kitchen table and opened the little boxes.

Samantha poked the chopsticks into the carton of sweet and sour pork and came out with a hunk of meat. "What did you two do today?"

"Dusty gave me a surfing lesson," Gillian said.

Dusty grinned at Gillian. "She needed it."

"It's not fair," Samantha whined. "I want a lesson."

"I don't know," he said.

"Please, please," Samantha begged.

"I promised Gillian I'd help her in the garden."

"You can do it tomorrow." Samantha grasped his hands and pulled him out of the chair. "I'll be ready in a jiffy." She raced up the stairs.

Dusty shrugged. "I guess I'm going surfing."

"I guess so," Gillian said, as she cleared the table.

Samantha and Dusty surfed until almost dark as Gillian changed back into her grubby clothes and pulled weeds. She felt miserable and she realized she was jealous. As she jabbed the screwdriver into the dirt and yanked each weed, she fumed.

Later as she lay in bed, she felt frustrated so she prayed, "Father, forgive me for my jealousy. I hate feeling jealous. Please change me." Her prayer didn't relieve her continued embittered thoughts as she stared at the ceiling. *I'm not sure if I even like him. Oh but I do like him. Am I just another in a long line of women to Dusty? Am I nothing special to him?* With the window open, the sheer curtains gracefully swayed in the breeze, the constant rumble of the surf lulled her to sleep.

The following morning, Gillian tromped out to raise the flag. As she approached the rose garden, Dusty popped up, a screw driver in one hand and the cardboard box, overflowing with weeds, in the other. "It's done. How does it look?" he asked, with his boyish grin.

Gillian stood like an ice sculpture. "Nice."

"Something wrong?"

"Nothing."

"Come on, where's your smile?" He held her chin in his hand.

Gillian jerked away from his touch. She didn't feel like smiling. She felt confused.

Chapter Eleven

Seated at the piano, Gillian played a medley of hymns as worshipers filed into the Chapel by the Sea. Before the service began, Josh and Samantha came in and strolled to the front of the church. They sat in the front pew. *Why am I so angry with them? They're my friends.* She prayed silently, *Lord soften my heart. I don't want to have a hard heart toward them. Fill me with your love so I can love as you do. Amen.*

Pastor Mike Richards stepped to the pulpit as Gillian took a seat in the pew next to Samantha, her opened Bible in her lap.

"Today's Scripture is Matthew 19:19," Pastor Mike said. "'Love your neighbor as yourself.' How can any of us love our neighbor, if we don't love ourselves? Have you done anything lately just for you? Some of you today are going to think I've gone off the deep end. You're wondering who will be the Sunday school teachers. Who will visit the sick? Who will lead our youth?"

"If each one of you only took on one ministry, everything would get done. Just one ministry. Some of you are here seven days a week. That's even more than I'm here. Stay home. Spend more time with your spouse. Spend more time with your family. Spend more time with Jesus."

"The purpose of the Garden of Eden was for God to have fellowship with Adam and Eve." He leaned forward on the pulpit. "Are you in fellowship with Him? Or are you so busy in ministry you don't have time for Him? There is no one more miserable than a Christian out of fellowship with Christ."

Pastor Mike placed his hands on either side of the pulpit. "Today I challenge you to serve in only one ministry. Those of you who are here more than two nights a week need to change your priorities and spend time in fellowship with God, your spouse, and your family."

Gillian observed his nod and stepped to the piano and played softly as he prayed.

The service over, Gillian continued to play while members exited the sanctuary or stayed to visit in clusters.

Gillian closed her music book and stepped down from the platform to where Josh and Samantha stood. "Josh and I are going to Ruby's for lunch. Come with us?" Samantha said.

"I'm visiting Mrs. Dodge...Gram's friend. Thanks anyway." Gillian smiled, masking her feelings.

Gillian waited until almost everyone was gone before she approached Pastor Mike, who stood at the back of the church. She offered her hand and he held it firmly yet gently between his own hands. "Thank you for all you do, Gillian."

"Pastor...Pastor Mike..."

"Yes."

"Can I meet with you this week?" Her heart pounded as she wrung her hands.

"Of course, call the office tomorrow and Lucy will set up an appointment for you." He released her hand and patted her on the back, his smile reassuring.

After Gillian asked to meet with him, she felt the heavy burden begin to lift.

*****

Gillian stepped through the automatic glass doors into Oceanview Terrace and entered room 16. Mrs. Dodge, who weighed not much more than Gillian, was in her bed, her silver hair framed her face as she lay on a pillow. Family pictures plastered the wall in front of her bed. The only items on her bedside table were a lamp, her well-worn Bible, a bound prayer journal, and a pencil. Gillian set her purse down on the straight-back wooden chair and went to the bed and touched Mrs. Dodge's hand laying on the thin blanket.

Mrs. Dodge opened her eyes. "Oh my dear, how lovely to see you."

Gillian wondered if it was a twinkle she saw behind the cloudy blue eyes.

"How have you been?" Gillian didn't remove her slender hand from Mrs. Dodge's boney, liver-spotted one.

"I had lots of visitors this week, and cards and letters." She pointed to a chest of drawers with cards displayed on top.

"You remember my grandson, Rory. He lives in Oregon now and he's a teacher, like you. He plans to visit me next month."

"How wonderful."

"Enough about me. Sit down." She patted the bed beside her. "Tell me all about yourself, my dear."

"I've been fixing up Gram's house. I even had a handyman build some new stairs down to the beach."

"What great fun your grandmother and I had with our children on the beach there." Mrs. Dodge looked off into the distance. "Your mother, always tan, wore the cutest, bright-colored swimsuits. Your grandmother made them for her, you know. Your mother was an instigator. She'd get my boys going, splashing water on them or she'd bury them in the sand, then she'd grab one of their prize possessions and run off. A real spit-fire your mother was."

"You and Gram were friends for a long time."

"Oh my, yes. Since grade school." Mrs. Dodge's cloudy blue eyes were moist. "I miss her."

"I know. So do I." Gillian felt the tears and tried to hold them back, but they would not obey.

"She loved you so much, my dear. And she was very proud of you." The older woman reached out her arms to welcome Gillian into them. And Gillian rested in the comfort of them for a long time. When Gillian sat back up on the bed, she wiped her cheeks with her fingertips.

The older woman looked quizzically at Gillian. "You look troubled, dear. What's bothering you?"

"My friends. They're talking behind my back... about... about... how I look."

"Do you mean about how terribly thin you are?"

"Yes." Gillian moved to a hard wooden chair. "I like being thin." She pulled her shoulders back. "I don't like being talked about behind my back."

"Would you listen if they said these things to your face?"

Gillian arched an eyebrow. *Probably not.* "What should I do?"

"Sometimes God uses His Word to speak to us, and sometimes it's a still small voice. And there are times when He uses others. Maybe God chose your friends to speak to you about what you're doing to your body. You see, it really isn't your body, my dear. It's God's temple. And, if I may be frank, you need to do something about it. God loves you and He has given you many talents. I know you serve Him because you love Him. Yet there is something you're keeping all to yourself."

"I never thought about my body being God's temple." Gillian mused. *Maybe God is already answering my prayer.*

Mrs. Dodge looked tired. Gillian stood and slung her purse over her shoulder.

"I pray for you every day, my dear." Mrs. Dodge laid her hand on her journal on the bedside table. "Your name is written in my prayer book."

"Thank you." Gillian bent down and kissed Mrs. Dodge's wrinkled cheek.

"Come anytime, dear."

"I will." Gillian reached the door and turned for one last look at the godly woman so frail. *God's not finished with her yet.*

Gillian left the nursing home feeling better. *I went to cheer up Mrs. Dodge and instead God spoke to me through her. Father, thank you for softening my heart towards Pastor Mike's sermon, and for Mrs. Dodge's prayers and wise counsel. Thank you for leading me to this saintly lady.*

She climbed into her VW and headed toward the beach house. On the way home, she stopped at the market for some groceries -- salad greens and fresh fruit, also bread and juice. She walked by the meat department and picked out some chicken. Then she stood in the bakery section with cakes, cookies, and pies surrounding her. She smiled as she picked out an enormous gooey chocolate cake on the shelf. *I'm going to shock them when they see me bring this home.*

At the check-out stand she watched as the grocery clerk ran the items over the scanner. The woman picked up the chocolate cake and looked at it longingly. "Yum. This sure looks good."

"Doesn't it though."

"Is it for something special?"

"Sort-of." Gillian's smile came from deep within her.

Soon, Gillian pulled onto the driveway, where a huge pile of tree and scrub clippings lay. The drone from a chain-saw buzzed in the background. Samantha pushed a wheelbarrow from the back of the house to the pile of debris. After she dumped it, she pulled off a gardening glove and wiped her brow.

Gillian got out of her VW and grabbed her purchases. "Wow. What's going on here?"

"When Josh and I got home, Dusty was pruning the trees and shrubs, so we decided to help him." Samantha pulled off the other glove. "I was about to go inside and get some ice water for us."

They entered the house. Gillian set the grocery bags on the kitchen counter and ran up the stairs to change. "I'll be right down," she called over her shoulder.

Chapter Twelve

Still in her PJ's, Gillian brewed a cup of tea and carried the warm mug into the living room. In the overstuffed chair, she tucked her knees under her and covered herself with Gram's afghan. Although she opened her Bible and devotional book to read the day's meditation and Scripture, her mind wandered. *Should I go up to the apartment and invite Dusty to church? Maybe I should just watch for him instead.* She turned back to her devotion, but kept picturing Dusty.

By ten o'clock she still hadn't decided how to approach him when she heard his Mustang pull out of the driveway.

"Rats. I missed him."

She put her cup in the sink and dashed upstairs to change into a pair of shorts and a T-shirt. She brushed and twisted her mane into a mass at the back of her head and clamped a giant-size barrette to hold it. Outside Gillian fruitlessly hacked at weeds when Dusty pulled in the driveway.

"Morning," he said as he grabbed the paint cans out of his trunk.

"Morning."

After he put them in the garage, he tramped over to Gillian and handed her the receipt.

She took off her gardening gloves. "I'll write you a check."

"No hurry." He grinned. "I'll be around." Dusty went to the garage and brought out the drop cloths, and began to cover the shrubs closest to the house.

Gillian stuffed the receipt into her pocket. "Let me help." She grabbed one end of the drop cloth. While covering the shrubs she yammered about non-essentials, everything except what was most important to her -- to invite Dusty to church. *What am I afraid of? He'll say no?*

Dusty traipsed to the garage and brought back an old heavy wooden ladder. He placed it against the house and checked to see it was sturdy before he climbed to the top of it and began to sand the chipped paint.

She shaded her eyes against the bright sunlight as she looked up at him. His mass of sun-bleached curls formed a halo around his head. Gillian bit her lower lip. "Would you like to go to church with me on Sunday?" She was glad he was above her so she didn't have to look into his warm eyes, because they unnerved her.

He didn't answer right away.

51

"I don't know." He ran his hand along the section he had just sanded, feeling the smoothness. "I'm not a church goer." He sanded the section on the other side of him. A mist of sawdust filtered down.

He came down from the ladder. "I'll make you a deal."

"What kind of deal?"

"I'll go to church with you if you go to an Adult Children of Alcoholics meeting with me. Josh wants you to go to a meeting, and with him gone all week, he asked me if I'd take you."

Gillian bristled at the betrayal. *It's Josh's fault.* As she started to walk away, she remembered her prayer. *Is this God's answer?*

"I can't fight both you and Josh. If it's the only way you'll come to church, it's a deal. I'll go to one of those ridiculous meetings with you." Gillian reached out and shook his hand.

Dusty examined her fingers. "I don't get how these small hands play such big music."

"It's not really my fingers. It's more like what's inside. It needs to get out. At least that's what Gram always told me, anyway." She slipped her hand away from his grasp.

"So, will you play some of the music...the music which needs to get out at church?"

"I guess." *Why did I say that? I always play the piano on Sunday.*

He grinned.

She went back to hoeing the weeds. *I get so flustered around him.*

*****

Gillian fumed when Dusty made a wrong turn while trying to find the Senior Center where the Adult Children of Alcoholics meeting was held. *I don't want to walk in late.*

They entered the room where a dozen people sat in a circle. Non-profit posters hung crooked on the stale, bland walls. A thin man in a blue stripped shirt got up and moved to another chair so Gillian and Dusty could sit together.

Gillian wanted to throw up. She crossed her arms and felt all eyes on her.

Dusty patted her leg reassuringly.

The leader, an obese woman wearing tight capris and a tent-like floral top said, "Welcome." Her small eyes in her puffy round face looked at Gillian and Dusty. "We've just started... so let's go around again and introduce ourselves." Gillian sank down on the hard folding chair and crossed her legs.

The person next to the leader took his cue and started. "I'm Brad, and I'm the adult child of an alcoholic."

"Hi Brad," the group chorused.

Next was a woman named Lorie.

Dusty was next. "I'm Dusty, and I'm... I'm just a visitor."

All eyes moved to Gillian.

"I'm Gillian," she whispered, unwilling, but as obedient as ever, "...and... I'm the child... of an... alcoholic."

As everyone introduced themselves, Gillian heard only her own words as they echoed in her head. *Why am I here? I don't need this.* The leader struggled to get up from the too small chair. As she walked toward Dusty and Gillian, her jowls jiggled. She handed them each a sheet of paper titled, "Common Behavior Characteristics of Adult Children." Everyone held a single sheet of paper in their hands. "Tonight we will discuss number thirteen -- 'We have difficulty following projects through from beginning to end.'" She smiled and her eyes disappeared in her cheeks.

While someone delivered a monologue on his experience of not being able to finish projects, Gillian scanned the rest of the list of characteristics; Low self-esteem, Isolate, Loyal...

Gillian placed the list on her lap and closed her mind to what those in the group said. She glanced at her watch then stared at the water-stained ceiling, bouncing her heels on the floor. *I don't belong here. I'm not like these people. Josh has gone too far. When can I get out of here?*

"Our higher power is different to each of us...God could be a woman in a pink dress," the leader said.

Startled from her thoughts, Gillian gasped, unable to believe what she'd heard.

While the others gathered around the coffee pot, holding paper cups in their hands, Gillian grabbed Dusty's arm. "Can we go? Please."

As they drove out of the parking lot, Gillian slumped in the seat and fumed. She watched the street lamps through the window. She was aware of Dusty and didn't know whether to be embarrassed or thankful he didn't fill the silence with meaningless chatter.

Dusty pulled into a parking space in front of a nearby café.

"What are you doing?" she asked.

"How about a cup of coffee?"

"I don't drink coffee. I'll have a cup of tea."

Inside the café, a waitress appeared and handed them menus. "Can I get you something to drink?"

"I'll have coffee," Dusty said.

"Do you have chamomile tea?" Gillian asked.

"I'll check."

Dusty leaned across the table toward Gillian. "How about a banana split?"

"No, thank you."

"Will you share one with me?" He looked over the top of the menu at her.

"No, I really don't want any ice cream." She looked at the menu, but wasn't reading it.

The server returned with their drinks. "I'll have a banana split," Dusty said, and handed the menu to the waitress.

When the waitress had left them, he said, "Okay, what's the matter?"

The anger, which she had held inside, burst like a dam. "I can't believe anyone could think of God as a woman in a pink dress! I know the only true God and *he* isn't a *she* in a pink dress."

"It is kind-of silly." He sipped his coffee. "Don't they call him Father in the Lord's Prayer?"

"Yes, they do. They call Him Father...not Mother. I wish I'd have thought of that. I'd have spoken up and told them my God isn't a woman and He doesn't wear a pink dress, either."

The waitress brought the banana split with chocolate syrup oozing over the top and placed it in front of Dusty.

He pushed it to the middle of the table. "Share it with me."

After more prodding, Gillian dipped her spoon into the chocolate covered ice cream. "I'm never going back there."

"Why?"

"Because of their idea of who God is, that's why."

"You need to look beyond what was said."

"I can't. It isn't who I believe God is. Besides, I'm not like them. I don't have difficulty finishing projects." She took another bite of ice cream. "I finished painting the kitchen," she said, with a mouth full of chocolate.

He smiled. "You haven't picked out the border yet."

"Because I haven't found what I want." Gillian blotted her mouth with a napkin and sipped her tea. "I went to one of those meetings. Now you have to come to church with us on Sunday. A deal's a deal." She laid her spoon down.

"You're right." He held out his hand.

She smiled, slipped her hand into his, and realized there was more to Dusty Bradshaw than being just a surfer. He was a hard worker and a sensitive man. Maybe she could even trust him.

Chapter Thirteen

Dusty lounged in front of the TV, mindlessly watching ESPN with Josh. Between them sat a huge plastic bowl of popcorn.

"I took Gillian to one of those 12-step meetings." Dusty rubbed his aching shoulder from sanding all week.

"How was it?" Josh stuffed a handful of popcorn in his mouth.

"A disaster." Dusty didn't want to have this conversation, but wanted to warn Josh rather than have him attacked by Gillian.

"How come?"

"The leader said God was a woman in a pink dress, and Gillian became irate." Dusty took a swig of his beer. "So much for going to one of those meetings."

"I don't blame her." Josh propped up his legs on the coffee table and crossed them at the ankles. "In case you haven't noticed, Gillian has a strong belief in God. So I can understand how she'd be upset."

"She did agree to a deal with me though."

"What kind of deal?" Josh asked.

"If she went to an ACA meeting, then I have to go to church with her on Sunday."

"Good for her."

"I guess it won't hurt me."

"You might even like it." Josh tossed a pillow at him.

Josh searched the empty fridge yet again. "What can one do with a half brick of cheese and ketchup?" He sliced a wedge of cheese and fell back on the couch. He plopped the last bite of cheese into his mouth. "When I was in Reno this week, I went to a 12-step meeting at a church. It was called New Hope. There wasn't any mention of God being a woman in a pink dress. I think I'll talk to my pastor and see if we could have a New Hope group at our church on Friday nights...so I can go to it."

Dusty picked at an irritating minute piece of popcorn shell wedged between his teeth. "I don't know if Gillian would ever step foot in one of those meetings again."

"I'll talk to her." Josh scratched his head. "Hopefully it won't go as badly as our date did."

*****

55

Still in her pajamas on Saturday morning, Gillian hummed as she fiddled around her newly redecorated kitchen. While searching the cupboards, she found some of her grandmother's treasures. She arranged several teapots of varied shapes, colors, and designs on the counter.

Pleased with what she had created, she went upstairs and gave herself a French manicure and a pedicure, using a pink polish. She painstakingly brushed the tips of her nails with the white polish and blew on them, waiting for them to dry. Gillian soaked in a bubble bath, and after stepping out of the tub and drying, she applied the green mask to her face. Feeling the refreshing goop work magic into her pores, she grabbed Debbie Macomber's new book and lay down on her bed to read.

The slamming of the door woke her. She checked the clock on the bedside table. *I must have dozed off.*

Samantha peeked into Gillian's room. "You missed a fantastic time." She did a double take. "It's best you stayed inside. You look positively frightening!"

"Thanks, Sam."

"Don't mention it. If your best friend won't tell you, who will?" Samantha walked away giggling. "I'm going to take a shower."

*****

Gillian rose earlier than usual Sunday morning and took pains getting ready for church. She washed and dried her thick mane, holding the blower in one hand and brushed her hair with the other. After she applied her make-up and styled her hair, she stepped into her favorite colorful floral sundress, with an eyelet bolero-style jacket.

She thought about Dusty as she spoke of God's love and forgiveness to the children in her Sunday school class. She felt Dusty's life was missing something and she knew what the something was. Like the children, Dusty needed a Savior, a personal relationship with his Creator. At the end of the Sunday school hour she saw the children off with a smile. "Have a good week. I'll see you next Sunday." When the last child was out of sight, she rushed to the sanctuary.

Gillian played a medley of hymns on the piano when Samantha, Josh, and Dusty arrived. They sat in a pew at the back of the church. Gillian's heart skipped a beat when she saw Dusty. She said a silent prayer, "Thank you, Lord."

After the announcements, music worship, and offering, Gillian walked to the back of the church, taking a seat next to Samantha.

Pastor Mike stepped behind the pulpit and began his sermon, "Nine-year-old Joey was asked by his mother what he had learned in

Sunday school. 'Well, Mom, our teacher told us how God sent Moses behind enemy lines on a rescue mission to lead the Israelites out of Egypt. When he got to the Red Sea, he had his engineers build a pontoon bridge and all the people walked across safely. Then, he used his walkie-talkie to radio headquarters for reinforcements. They sent bombers to blow up the bridge and all the Israelites were saved.' His mother replied, 'Now, Joey, is that really what your teacher taught you?' 'Well, no, Mom. If I told it the way the teacher did, you'd never believe it!'"

Laugher reverberated through the sanctuary. When it faded, Pastor Mike continued, "Joey didn't think his mother would believe the truth. There are folks who don't believe the truth concerning God's grace either. They find it hard to believe God gave his only Son to suffer and die for sinners. Yet it's what he did out of his abounding love for us."

Gillian did a victory dance in her heart and her head when Pastor Mike spoke on God's grace for Dusty's first visit. She said a silent prayer. *Please God, soften Dusty's heart to hear and receive your free gift of salvation during the altar call at the end of the service.*

She returned to the piano and watched Dusty as the congregation sang, "Amazing Grace." She prayed while her fingers played the old hymn from memory. Dusty didn't step forward. He stood motionless at the back of the church between Josh and Samantha.

After the service, Gillian rushed to Dusty's side. At the front door of the sanctuary, Pastor Mike reached out his sun-tanned hand to Dusty.

"Pastor Mike, I'd like you to meet Dusty," Gillian said.

"It's nice to meet you, Dusty. I understand from Gillian and Josh you're a surfer. We'll have to catch some waves together sometime," Pastor Mike said.

Dusty returned his handshake. "Sounds good."

Later, unable to wait another minute, Gillian nudged Dusty in the donut line during the coffee and fellowship time after the service. "What did you think?"

"About what?" Dusty grinned.

"About the service?"

"It was church." He popped a donut hole in his mouth. "It really hasn't changed much since my grandparents took me when I was ten." After taking a swig of coffee from a paper cup, he added, "I feel closer to God when I'm riding a wave."

That's God's creation. You can like God's creation, and enjoy it, and be thankful for it, but it isn't God. You need to have a relationship with the Creator, not his creation. At least he came to church. Maybe today wasn't God's timing. She'd have to wait on God's mastery, which wasn't always the easiest thing for her to do.

At home, Gillian and Samantha changed their clothes and were waiting down at the beach when Josh and Dusty arrived in their swim trunks, carrying drinks, burgers, and fries from In-N-Out.

"I'm famished." Josh handed out the burgers. He poured the fries into the cardboard box and set it in the middle of the foursome. "Dig in," he said.

Dusty handed a diet Pepsi to Gillian.

Gillian nibbled her burger as the others devoured theirs. Scanning the horizon, she scrutinized the waves for their power over Dusty.

Within a few minutes, they consumed the food, stretched out on their beach towels, and soaked in the rays on the beautiful, sunny California day. Gillian gently stroked the warm sand with her toes. The heat from the sun massaged her tired back.

"Well, I've waited long enough," Dusty said. He ran up the stairs, and soon returned with his surfboard. "Anyone for another surfing lesson?"

"Sure," Samantha said, jumping up. "Josh, you coming?"

"Not right now," Josh said.

Dusty and Samantha ran into the white foamy water and soon she was on top of Dusty's surfboard with him beside her.

Gillian turned over and lay on her stomach. Josh did the same. Gillian laid her head on her folded arms and imagined what was happening out in the water between Dusty the encourager and instructor and Samantha the giggling flirt.

Josh played with the sand. "Pastor Mike plans to start a new ministry. It's called New Hope. It's like the meeting you went to with Dusty. Pastor Mike--"

"Don't remind me," Gillian interrupted.

"Dusty told me about what happened. I'm sorry. New Hope is different. It's based on Scripture." He turned on his side and faced her. With his elbow on his towel, he leaned his head on his hand. "I went to one of the meetings when I was in Reno last week." He brushed some sand off his towel. "Pastor Mike has wanted to start this ministry for a long time. He doesn't want it on church property. He thinks it would be better to have it in a home...for people's privacy. I told him the meeting can be in the apartment on Friday nights...so I can attend. He thought it was a good idea. After I thought about the living room's size and lack of furniture, I was wondering if you'd have it at your house?"

"What?" She raised her head off her arms. "I don't think so." She laid her head back down. "Get someone else. I'm already teaching Sunday school and playing the piano." She added smugly, "In fact, Pastor Mike advocates sharing ministry instead of the same people doing it all. And I agree with him."

"You won't have to do anything. Pastor Mike said he'd lead the group."

"Just clean the house." She finally looked at him and noticed his pleading eyes. *He really does care about me. Not even Josh knows how much despair is huddled in the corner of my heart.* She lowered her eyes again.

"People don't care about what kind of a housekeeper you are." He scooped sand into a mound and patted it as the stray pieces tumbled down. "Will you at least think about it?"

"I'll think about it."

As Josh let sand flow between his fingers, Gillian's imagined what it would be like having one of those meetings in her house. *Maybe I'll let Pastor Mike use my house for meetings, but I won't say, "My name is Gillian, and I'm..."*

Josh jumped up. "Time to catch a wave." He offered her his hand. "You coming?"

"Not right now."

"Please." He stuck out his lower lip pouty like.

She laughed. "You look pitiful, but I'm not going to change my mind. Go."

He turned and jogged away.

Later, Gillian was awakened when Samantha flopped down on her towel next to her. "It was the most fun I've ever had," Samantha gushed.

When Gillian turned over and sat up, Dusty grabbed her hand and pulled her to her feet. "Your turn." Dusty picked her up and threw her over his shoulder. He trudged through the sand and into the water where Josh kept the surfboard from floating away. She yelled, pounded his back, and kicked her legs. Dusty put her on the top of the surfboard at the front and he lay on the back of it behind her, paddling out beyond the waves.

Gillian's heart raced. Once the shock of the cold water subsided, they glided as the board sliced through the water. While Dusty's powerful strokes paddled out to deeper water, she didn't dare look back at him, but faced the horizon. They flew through the water. It was smoother than an arpeggio, more powerful than a crescendo. It was more sublime even than Beethoven's 9. In the midst of God's majestic ocean, she was enveloped and surrounded by God's power and beauty. It was her glimpse of eternity. She'd always marveled at the truth of God's promises and of heaven having no end. As Dusty's arm brushed hers, she was reminded with urgency how much he needed God.

Holding the board, Dusty's patience had no end as he instructed her on how to surf. For some reason she couldn't concentrate. She only wanted to roll with the power of God's sea.

Gillian was lost in the endless moment as Dusty turned the surfboard sideways and shared it side by side with her, their elbows rested on the board and looking out at the horizon, their legs dangling in the cool water. *Oh God, You are majestic!*

*****

Gillian sat at the table on the patio, a towel wrapped around her. Her wet hair was full of sand. Dusty straddled the picnic bench, facing her. "Now you look like a real surfer girl." He brushed some sand off the end of her ponytail.

As the screen door slid open, Gillian glanced up as Samantha stepped onto the patio. She wore white shorts and a tight black T-shirt with a plunging neckline. Her one-inch heeled gold sandals clicked on the patio. She carried a green salad and Josh followed with a butcher knife in his hand and a watermelon tucked under his arm. Samantha smelled of lavender as she placed the salad in the middle of the table. She smiled. "I see you two didn't dress for dinner." Then she giggled, turned, and went back inside the house.

Dusty whispered in Gillian's ear, "Were we supposed to dress for dinner?"

Gillian laughed.

While Josh speared the barbecued chicken from the outdoor grill and piled it on a platter, Samantha returned with sourdough bread.

After dinner, Gillian licked the barbecue sauce off her fingers. "Josh, I've made a decision."

"Yeah." Josh yawned. "What about?"

"You can have the New Hope meeting at my house."

"Thanks, Gilly,"

"Friday nights, right?"

"Uh-huh." Josh yawned again. "I'll let you know when it's supposed to start."

Samantha covered her mouth to stifle a yawn, "Stop it, Josh. It's catching."

Josh stood. "I think I'll hit the hay. Night, everyone."

"Night, Josh," they echoed.

Gillian eyed the dirty dishes. "It's late. I'll stack these in the sink and wash them in the morning."

Samantha got up from the bench. "Thanks, Gilly." She flipped her hair behind her ear. "Since I'm a working girl, I'd better get my beauty sleep. Ta-ta." She waved.

With the sun down, the air had turned chilly and although the tiki torches offered a nice touch to a lovely evening, they gave little warmth.

Still wearing her damp swimsuit, Gillian shivered, then stood and began to clear the table.

Dusty stacked and carried a pyramid of dirty dishes into the kitchen. "What's a New Hope meeting?" he asked.

She rolled her eyes. "One of those 12-step meetings."

"Oh."

She ran hot water in the sink and added dish-washing soap. "Josh said it's based on Scripture."

"Well good. I'm glad..."

"I'm just offering my house." She turned off the water. "Only the house."

Dusty didn't say anything, and she didn't feel unnerved around him anymore. She felt comfortable.

She shivered. "I think I'm going to take a hot bath."

"Then I guess it's time for me to go."

"Thanks for helping clear the table, Dusty." She grabbed a dishtowel and dried her hands. "Thanks for... today." Her eyes met his.

He reached out and took her hand. "Good night."

Still holding his hand, she walked him to the front door. "Night."

After closing the door, she locked it, turned off lights, and climbed the stairs, where she ran a hot bath and daydreamed about another day with Dusty. "Please, Lord, soften Dusty's heart towards you."

Chapter Fourteen

Dusty peered out the living room window of his apartment, a coffee mug in his hand. He watched below for Gillian to appear on her daily trek to the flagpole. He planned to meet her there and offer to help her with the dishes stacked in her kitchen sink from the night before.

While he waited, he pondered the losses he'd suffered. He had loved Jennie and believed they would spend their lives together until her parents sabotaged their future together. He was ready and able to fight for her, but it was Jennie who faltered, allowing them to interfere. In the end, they wore her down. She wasn't strong enough to go against their wishes. He sipped his coffee. Could it really be five years ago he lost Jennie?

He ran his hand through his mass of sun-bleached curls, remembering. Two years later Pop died, leaving him grief stricken. Now he floundered, living day to day, without direction or purpose.

He moved to the kitchen and dumped his cold coffee down the sink, then poured himself a second cup and returned to stand at the window. He scanned the low silver horizon and sighed at the breadth of it.

His thoughts turned to Gillian. She wasn't the same uptight person he met the day he moved to Reagan Beach. He'd grown to admire her for pulling herself up by her bootstraps so to speak. She was a survivor. And he liked her determination to restore her grandmother's house. Once she decides to do something, nothing is going to stop her. Although he didn't share her strong belief in God, he respected her faith. She lived a Christian life others only talked about.

She came into view as she walked to the flagpole, jogging him from his reverie. He set his coffee mug in the kitchen sink and descended the stairs, leaping the last three.

He approached her as she strolled back to the house. "Good morning."

"Morning, Dusty."

"We really left a mess last night. I'll help you clean it up."

She smiled. "Okay. I'll wash and you can dry."

"Um, how about I wash and you dry -- since you know where everything goes." He followed her into the house.

"I guess I can go along with it."

He drained the cold water and refilled the kitchen sink with hot soapy water, dipping his hands into the warm suds. "I'm glad you decided to have the New Hope meetings here."

"Why?"

Dusty chose his words carefully. "You may... get something from them."

"I'm not doing it for me. I'm doing it for Josh."

"I know. And I'm sure he appreciates it." He put a clean, wet plate in the drainer.

The only sounds were of running water and cupboard doors closing as Dusty washed and Gillian dried and put dishes away.

Gillian broke the silence. "Did your grandfather teach you how to wash dishes?" She grinned at him, eyes laughing.

"Nah. It was my mom." He flicked soapy water in her hair as she ducked and squealed.

"Do you get along with her?"

"Mom's my buddy, but it was time for me to leave. I'm glad she married Matt." He wiped one stray bubble from her hair and changed the subject. "I plan to finish prepping the house for paint today."

"After I have my devotions, I'll help." She frowned. "I hope it won't be as messy as stripping wallpaper."

"It won't. You can tape newspaper on the windows while I sand." He dried his hands on the end of the dishtowel she held.

"Okay."

Dusty leaned against the counter watching her put the last of the clean dishes away. *I'm ready for a relationship. The past is gone. I've grieved much too long over my losses. I want to live again. I'll never forget Jennie or Pop. They're a part of the man I am.*

He'd rehearsed what he was going to say and now he bolstered up enough courage to say it. "I'd like to take you out to dinner Saturday night."

"The four of us?"

"No. Just you." Hopeful, he searched her expression. *Please say yes.* "Well not 'just' you. You."

"You mean like a date?"

He grinned. "Yes. Like a date."

"I'd like that."

*****

After he left, she rushed to have her devotions, her ponytail dancing. *I've got a date. I've got a date.* She plopped down in the comfy chair and opened her devotion book to where she had stuck in the

63

bookmark the day before. She scanned the verse and stopped abruptly. She reread John 15:16 slowly, "You did not choose me, but I chose you." She read it again. Oh Lord, she prayed, please help Dusty find and accept you."

By three o'clock, Gillian had covered the bottom floor windows with newspaper and Dusty had scraped and scraped for hours, stopping only for a quick tuna sandwich Gillian had made for him.

Dusty wiped his brow. "We got a lot done today. I think we deserve some R and R."

"Sounds good to me." She pushed stray hair out of her face with the back of her hand.

"How about another surfing lesson?"

"Do you think I need it?"

"Oh yeah." He grinned.

"You're the teacher. If you really think I need it."

"I'll meet you down at the beach in ten minutes."

She watched him toss the masking tape and other supplies in the garage and take the steps two at a time up to the apartment.

After changing into her swimsuit, she waded and jumped breakers out to where he was waiting. He floated gently on his surfboard. Gillian took notice of his sure, gentle strokes, and thought about how he loved his mother and Pop. And she thought of Gram and felt Gram's limitless love buoying her to Dusty's side. She wanted to surf with him because she wanted to share this part of his life and, more than anything, she wanted him to know God's love.

After playing with Dusty in the warm sun, sand and water, she mused. *This summer promises more than I could have ever dreamed.*

Arriving at the top of the cliff, Samantha greeted them. "It looks like you two had fun." Samantha frowned. "Have you thought about dinner?"

Gillian giggled. "Not really."

"Well, I'm starved." Samantha punched her fists on her hips.

Dusty brushed the sand out of his hair. "Me too."

"There are leftovers in the fridge," Gillian said.

"I can bring some leftover pizza," Dusty offered.

"Ugh, not pizza again," Gillian moaned.

"You've got to be kidding. It's a staple for us guys." Dusty tweaked her nose.

The next day, Dusty and Gillian worked on the house. They each held a bucket of paint in one hand and a paintbrush with the other. Dusty, perched on the ladder, painted the top part of the house while Gillian painted the lower half. With each stroke, Gillian saw the old pain and hurt obscured by something new. Fresh. Shiny. She worked tirelessly, happily.

Above her, Dusty crooned a little off key, "Little surfer, little one, made my heart come all undone. Do you love me, do you surfer girl..."

She smiled, but she couldn't look at him.

Chapter Fifteen

The following Friday morning, while Dusty worked on the outside of the house, Gillian kept busy on the inside. She scrubbed the bathrooms in preparation for the New Hope meeting. *I'm doing this for you, Josh. I don't understand why you think you need a group. You were so lucky to have both your parents. So what if your dad spent so much time at work. Isn't working what dads are supposed to do. Provide for their families, not abandon them?* The more she thought, the more vigorously she scrubbed.

"Why am I cleaning the upstairs bathroom? No one will come up here." She laughed. "I'm ridiculous." She turned on the faucet and rinsed the soapy residue down the drain. After giving the mirror a once over with Windex and a paper towel, she descended the stairs and stowed the caddy of cleaning supplies in the broom closet. She pulled out the vacuum and plugged it in. Then she peeked out the window in hopes of seeing Dusty, but he was nowhere in sight. *He's probably on the other side of the house.* The vacuum hummed as she ran it back and forth, back and forth over the carpet. Thoughts of the meeting and what to expect consumed her as she cleaned.

With the house cleaned, she showered, washed and dried her hair, carefully applied make-up, and brushed and styled her hair. She pulled on a pair of turquoise capris and a colorful floral print blouse. After searching for Dusty, she found him near the top of the ladder on the north side of the house, painting. "Hey! You want a BLT?" she called.

"Sounds good."

"It'll be ready in about five minutes."

The table was set with yellow gingham placemats. In the center was a healthy Chinese evergreen in one of her grandmother's antique ceramic pots. Gillian placed the bacon, wrapped like a mummy in paper towels, into the microwave and popped the wheat bread into the toaster. She was slicing the beefsteak tomato when Dusty tapped on the screen door off the patio. "Come in," she called.

When he entered the kitchen, Gillian noticed while he had been painting, he was shirtless. Now, he wore a faded navy blue tank top. Dusty sat at the kitchen table with a bottle of Gatorade in his hand. "So tonight's the night you've been dreading?"

"How'd you know I'm dreading it?" She cut the sandwiches in half, placed them on plates, and brought them to the table.

"I guess I'm getting to know you."

"Let's just say I'm not looking forward to it." She took a bite of her sandwich.

"I think dread is still more accurate."

"You're right." She blotted the sides of her mouth with a napkin.

He nodded toward the centerpiece. "I see you've become a regular Martha Stewart."

"Not really." She sipped her iced tea. "In fact, I'd never want to be her."

"Why?"

"Her husband left her."

"What about all her money?" He leaned back in his chair and took a gulp of Gatorade.

"Money isn't important to me."

He grinned approvingly at her. "I heard the vacuum humming all morning. The house looks great."

"Thanks."

"So, while I'm slaving away in the hot sun, what's your plan for this afternoon?"

"Well, after I clean up our lunch dishes, I plan to spend some R and R time playing the piano." She wiped her hands on her napkin and placed it on her empty plate.

"Sounds good." He scooted his chair back and stood. "I think I'll move the ladder to the west side of the house so I can listen to you play while I work." He carried his plate to the counter. "Thanks for lunch."

*****

The music she created soothed her anxiousness about the pending meeting, but later the uncomfortable feeling returned as she hid behind her smile. She opened the door for Pastor Mike and helped him set up the half dozen folding chairs he had brought. Once they had formed a circle in the living room, he went back to his car for a box of materials and met Dusty carrying a paint can to the garage. "Hello, Dusty," Pastor Mike said.

Dusty wiped his hand on his cutoffs, and then clasped Pastor Mike's hand.

Pastor Mike shaded his eyes from the sun. "Monday is my day off. You available to go surfing?"

Gillian joined them in the driveway.

"I'd like to... but..." Dusty glanced at Gillian like a little boy who needed permission. "...I don't know if I can... I'm in the middle of painting the house."

Gillian laughed. "Don't let it stop you."

"Okay. Sure, I'm available," Dusty said.

"Great! Eight o'clock okay?" Pastor Mike hoisted the box of materials from his trunk.

"Eight's fine with me."

"See you then." Pastor Mike and Gillian headed for the front door of the cottage while Dusty stored the paint can in the garage.

Soon a dozen folks gathered. Gillian knew some of them, and some she didn't.

Josh's cleared his throat. "My name is Josh. The reason I'm here is... to work through... how I feel about being neglected emotionally by my dad. He was a great dad in many ways...but...he was married to his job. He was a workaholic. He provided for us... and he never abused any of us verbally... or physically. So in many ways I am luckier than a lot of people. I just need to work through the steps of recovery... forgive my dad...and get on with my life." He leaned back in the folding chair.

Feeling compassion, Gillian put her hand on his leg, and he put his hand over hers, grasping it with his sweaty palm.

While others shared their innermost pain, Gillian rehearsed what she would say only if and when she was ready. *My name is Gillian, and I'm the adult child of an alcoholic. When this group first started meeting, I was unable to share. I was frozen in my seat and afraid to talk. I felt like I had this scar and if I said anything it would open and puss would ooze out, and it would keep oozing and never stop. So instead of telling my story, I listened to everyone else, cried with them, and remembered my own shame and pain. It isn't easy to share my feelings. I've kept everything on the inside. I thought I was fine because I had Gram. I know she loved me and she gave me a good home. I guess I never realized until now how my mother's drinking and being abandoned by her and my father really did have an effect on me.* She forced back the threatening sobs. *I can't share. Not now. Maybe never.*

*****

On Saturday, although she kept an eye out for him, she didn't see Dusty all day. Her thoughts about what it would be like on a date with him consumed her. Whenever she heard a noise outside, she raced to the window and peered out in hopes of seeing him, only to be disappointed. She took her time getting ready. After giving herself a facial, manicure and pedicure, she soaked in a bubble bath. Soft music played and lighted candles encircled the bathtub. It was a luxury she seldom afforded herself. With a smile she remembered him singing "Surfer Girl".

Gillian's black halter dress shimmered over her thin, tan frame. Her hair was swept up in a cascade of curls, little wisps lay gently on her smooth neck. Hearing a rap on the door, Gillian opened it. Dusty stood on the porch. He'd had a haircut and wore a short sleeve white silk shirt and tan slacks. Now Gillian saw what Samantha had seen the first day they met. It was true -- Dusty was gorgeous. Without thinking she said, "Wow!"

He laughed. "My mother always said I cleaned up well." His eyes sparkled.

"Your mother's right."

Later, they sat at a table for two at the Chart House and talked over salads. "Do you date a lot?" he asked.

"Not really. I dated in college, but nothing serious." She sipped her water.

"What about Josh?"

"Josh? Josh is a good friend. And he's a Christian." She was thoughtful. "I'd never marry someone who wasn't a Christian." *He didn't say anything about marriage? I'm such a klutz. He must think I'm ridiculous.*

"I've heard some marriages start as friendships."

"That may be true, but unless I'm living in a fantasy world, I want more than friendship."

"Like what? Do you want your heart to go pitter-patter when he's near?" He grinned.

"Yes. I do." She smiled. "What about you. Do you have someone in Santa Cruz waiting for you?"

"Not anymore. I was engaged to my high school sweetheart, but her parents jinxed it. Their exact words were 'not good enough.'"

He buttered his bread. "They didn't want their daughter to marry someone who worked with his hands."

"You're kidding." She held her fork above her plate. "You do beautiful work."

"Thanks."

The waiter approached, removed their salad plates, and put juicy steaks in front of them. "Will there be anything else?"

"Could we have some more bread?" Dusty gestured toward the empty basket.

The waiter left, carrying the breadbasket.

"What was I saying?" Dusty asked.

"You were talking about your fiancée's parents jinxing your engagement."

"Right. It was five years ago." He cut a bite of steak. "I've dated a few times since then, but I've never been interested in anyone. No one's been able to come close to Jennie."

Gillian heard the sadness in his voice. "Her parents were mistaken. There's nothing wrong with being a craftsman, and you're a good one. The stairs you constructed are well built, and I could see the pride you took in creating them. I've got the best steps leading to the beach in all of Reagan, probably even the best on the coast."

"Well, I wouldn't go so far as to say that, but thanks." He smiled at her with his penetrating hazel eyes. "My mom wasn't disappointed. She never thought Jennie was the one for me. She said I deserved the kind of love she and my dad had." He pulled an old wrinkled photo out of his wallet and handed it to Gillian. "It's my parent's wedding picture."

"You look like your dad."

"Everyone says I do."

"Your mother's beautiful."

"She still is."

Gillian gazed at the photo. *I want to wear a wedding gown like this one...and have an outdoor wedding beside the rose garden at Gram's house.* She handed the photo back to him. "I'm sorry. I was lost in thought."

"Happy thoughts I hope." He put the photo back in his wallet.

"They were."

"Do you want to tell me about them?"

"Maybe another time."

She avoided his eyes. He is so much more than a surfer. *He's sensitive, especially when he talks about his mother and Pop. Yet... I'm still not sure if I can trust him.*

When the evening came to an end, he walked her to the front porch and before she opened the door, she turned to face him. "I had a--"

He put his arm around her waist and pulled her to him. She was captivated by the wonderful scent of the masculine musk he wore. At first he kissed her lightly on the mouth. When she didn't pull away, he kissed her a second time, this time more passionately. His arms lingered around her waist as they stood on the porch.

Before sleep came, she thought about the evening. *Dusty Bradshaw you not only clean up well, but you're a great kisser too. I bet your mother doesn't know everything about you.* She giggled and pulled the comforter over her head.

Chapter Sixteen

At eight o'clock sharp on Monday morning, Dusty watched Pastor Mike, a tall, tan, muscular surfer, descend the stairs, carrying his surfboard. Looking like a natural athlete, he waded into the water and, with long powerful strokes, paddled out to where Dusty sat on his board.

Reaching Dusty, Pastor Mike asked, "How is it?"

"Pretty calm," Dusty said. "I see you have a hybrid fish. Do you like it?"

"Don't know. Today's the first time."

"I thought about getting one, but I'm happy with my board. It's sort of like a comfortable pair of cutoffs -- why change a good thing?"

They caught a few small waves, but most of the morning they sat in the deep water side by side startling their surfboards, and waiting.

Pastor Mike broke the silence. "How long you been surfing?"

"Since I was a kid. My grandfather taught me."

"It was my dad who taught me. We lived in Santa Monica and he would take me to Muscle Beach every chance he got." Pastor Mike looked off in the distance. "In fact, he even saved my life." He didn't wait for Dusty to ask what happened, but went right on with his story. "My dad is a lot of fun. He's also strict. So I knew I'd better obey him. One time we were swimming in a riptide, but I didn't know it. Dad said, 'just float for a while'. I didn't ask why, I just did what he said. After an eternity of floating in the water, Dad said, 'Swim to shore as fast as you can -- like the Devil's after ya.' Well. I didn't question him. I just did what he said. When we reached shore, we both fell onto the beach exhausted. He told me we'd been in a riptide." Pastor Mike was thoughtful. "If he had told me when we were in it, I don't know if I would have been afraid or not. I like to think he knew what was best for me."

They bobbed on their surfboards as Pastor Mike continued, "I trusted Dad with my life." He faced Dusty. "I think of God as being a lot like my dad. He disciplines me, and he's my best friend too. I trust him with my life."

"I trusted my grandfather," Dusty said, and then clammed up. He did not feel comfortable telling Pastor Mike he blamed God for taking his father and grandfather away from him. He didn't think anyone would understand how he felt. No one, except... Gillian. She'd understand. Pastor Mike did not pursue the subject. Had he taken the clue from Dusty's silence? They ended the morning by riding a wave into shore together, and then climbed the sturdy stairs, carrying their surfboards at their sides.

Pastor Mike strapped his board to the rack on the top of his SUV then shook Dusty's hand. "Thanks for surfing with me today."

"Too bad the surf wasn't better to try out your new board."

"Next time."

*****

Gillian pulled into the driveway and parked next to where Dusty was meticulously rubbing paste into his surfboard. "How was surfing with Pastor Mike?"

"Okay." He stopped what he was doing and grabbed grocery bags from the VW and carried them to the house.

"Just okay?"

"The surf wasn't up. So he talked and I listened."

"What'd he talk about?" Gillian asked as she placed lettuce and tomatoes in the sink to be washed.

"About him and his dad being caught in a riptide. How he trusted him with his life, and how he thinks of God being like his dad and how he trusts God. I stopped listening to him when he said God has a plan for my life."

"Why?"

With his head down he leaned against the counter. "Because... I blame God for taking my dad before I ever had a chance to know him... and then he took my Pop too."

Gillian thought about Dusty being big and strong, and yet so vulnerable. *He needs my Jesus. But his heart is so hard toward God. She said a silent prayer. Lord, please melt his heart toward you and give me the words to minister to him.* "Do you know about the story of Jesus dying on the cross?"

He looked up. "Yeah."

"Jesus said, 'Father, why have you forsaken me?' Although Jesus knew what was about to happen, he doubted God's plan." She took Dusty's rough hand and led him into the living room and they sat down on the sofa. "We don't always understand why bad things happen, but we can trust giving God control of our lives. He knows what is best for us. Just like Pastor Mike knew his dad knew what was best for them when they were in the riptide." As they held hands she rubbed her thumb back and forth across his hand.

"I don't understand your faith. Was it God's plan for your parents to abandon you?"

72

"I don't believe it was God." She chose her words carefully. "God gives us a free will. It was my parents' choice to... abandon... me. I believe it was God's plan for Gram to raise me."

"Yet... he took her from you too."

She stopped rubbing her thumb across his hand. "I miss her terribly, yet I don't question God's timing." Her voice cracked and the tears spilled over. "I believe she's in heaven and I'll join her someday."

He gently wiped her tears with his fingertips. "You have a strong faith, and I'm happy for you. I only wished I had your faith."

Chapter Seventeen

Dressed in floral print capris pants and a yellow T-shirt, Gillian stood in the living room at the bottom of the stairs. "Let's go!" she called up the stairs.

"Okay. Okay. Hold your horses." Samantha came skipping down the stairs and joined Gillian at the bottom. Her hair was styled in a smooth pageboy and tucked behind her ears. She wore navy shorts with a red, white, and blue paisley blouse. It matched the trim on the cuffs of her shorts.

"Hold my horses?" Gillian giggled. "I haven't heard that since I was a little girl."

Samantha smiled. "I think my grandpa used to say it when he'd get impatient with someone."

"Are you impatient with me?" Gillian grabbed her car keys from the peg next to the front door.

"I think it's the other way around. For some reason, I think you're impatient with me. What's the rush anyway?"

Gillian put on her sunglasses, and with car keys in hand led the way to her VW bug. "There's just so much to do to get ready for Royal Family Kids' Camp...and I thought we agreed we'd go shopping this morning -- and it's already noon."

There was no sign of Dusty and Josh as Gillian backed her car out of the driveway and sped down the street.

"Did you bring the list?" Samantha asked as she pulled down the visor and checked her make-up, hair, and her teeth in the mirror.

"Got it." Gillian pulled onto the highway and headed north. "I thought we'd hit the Discovery Shop first. I need to find a dress to wear for the tea party at camp."

"What about all the other stuff we need?"

"Everything's on the list." Gillian was thoughtful. "I thought about taking one of the pretty teapots from Gram's collection, but I'd feel terrible if anything happened to it, so I think I'll look for a teapot too."

Gillian found a parking place close to the thrift store and once inside they sashayed around merchandise racks until they found the formal dresses. Most of the wedding dresses were in small sizes and Samantha gushed over several of them. "Look at this one," Samantha said as she held one then another.

Gillian calculated in her head the cost of the secondhand gowns. She knew the purchase of even one was beyond her budget, even if it was for a good cause. She continued to search for one less expensive. Not finding one under fifty dollars, she moved on to another display. Half way down the rack she found a long light blue two piece with beading all over the top. She pulled it off the rack to get a better look. "Sam, look!" She held up her find. The beading was in the design of teapots. "Can you believe it? Who would ever think of making a dress with teapots all over it?"

"What a hoot!"

"I can't believe it!" Gillian searched for the price tag and discovered it was in her price range.

"How much is it?"

"Fourteen dollars," Gillian said. She was both surprised and delighted with the price.

"You going to get it?"

"I think so. I'm going to try it on." Gillian went in search of the dressing rooms.

Samantha went back to dragging the hangers from right to left as she continued on her mission of finding a dress for herself. Soon she had several draped over her arm as she went to find the dressing rooms and Gillian. "Gilly, you here?"

"Here." Gillian stepped out of the cubical and turned around for Samantha to see the full effect of the teapot dress. "What do you think?"

"It's perfect."

They both giggled as Gillian stepped back into the dressing room to take off the dress and Samantha unloaded her find in the adjoining stall. While Samantha tried on the assortment of wedding dresses and prom dresses, Gillian dressed and went to find a shopping cart. She put the teapot dress in the basket and pushed it back and forth down the aisles with assorted dishware when Samantha joined her with another shopping cart. Gillian held up a round-shaped teapot with delicate blue flowers painted on it. "Look...and there are six cups and saucers to match. Just what we need."

"Let's get it."

"I don't know how much it costs." Gillian searched for the price tag.

"It doesn't matter. I'll pay for it."

"It's fifteen dollars."

"For everything?" Samantha asked.

"Uh-huh."

"What a deal!" Samantha began taking the tea set down from the shelf and putting it into Gillian's shopping cart because her cart was overflowing with satin, lace, and net. The teapot dress lying in the bottom of Gillian's shopping cart became a cushion of protection for the china.

After strolling down more isles in search of other finds, they went to the checkout counter. "May I speak to the manager, please?" Gillian said.

An efficient clerk with wire rimmed glasses perched on the end of her nose said, "I'm sorry she isn't here today."

"Maybe you can help me." Gillian handed her a Royal Family Kids' Camp business cards. "My name is Gillian Grant and my friend and I are volunteers for a camp for abused and neglected children. I'd like to know if you would be willing to donate these items to the camp."

"I'm sorry, but I don't have the authority," the clerk said.

"It's okay." Samantha nudged Gillian aside and stepped up to the counter. "I'll pay for them." She rummaged around in her huge straw purse and eventually pulled out her checkbook and a pen.

"I'll pay for part of it." Gillian reached into her purse.

"I've got it," Samantha said, then added, "you can get the other stuff we need."

They left the thrift store and stuffed the mountains of netting, lace, and satin in Gillian's yellow VW bug and headed for the dollar store. Gillian ran in and picked up some blue party napkins and returned to the car were Samantha waited.

"I'm starved. How about a salad at McDonalds?" Samantha asked.

"Okay...but only if I can treat."

"Okay. I won't argue with you," Samantha agreed.

They found a table next to the window, sat down and unwrapped their plastic utensils. Poking a straw into the large iced tea, Gillian said, "I'm so excited. With Gram's blue and white checked tablecloth and the blue artificial flowers in a tall white bud vase, everything is going to look perfect. We'll use the picnic table beside our cabin."

Samantha's fork hovered over her chicken salad. "My mother saved all of my prom dresses." In between bites of salad, Samantha continued. "I think I'll wear the pink one I wore to the prom our junior year. Do you remember it?"

"Of course. I remember all of them...even the white strapless one you wore our freshmen year when you had boobs and I didn't."

Samantha grinned. "Things haven't changed much," she said good-naturedly.

"They're coming back."

"You mean their bigger than a twenty-eight triple A?"

"Yes." Gillian smiled, and said seriously, "Anorexia had an adverse effect on them, didn't it." She said it more like a statement rather than a question.

"I'm glad you're doing something about it."

"Me too." Gillian stopped eating and looked into Samantha's eyes. "Thanks for being my friend and helping me see what I was doing to myself."

"Sure. What friends are for? Right?"

"Right." Gillian changed the subject. "The girls are going to love the dresses you bought today."

"I think I'll donate all my formals to camp." Samantha stabbed a piece of lettuce. "They are going to love them." She agreed with Gillian.

"I talked to the camp cook and she said we can use the kitchen one day to bake the cookies for our tea party." Gillian absentmindedly twirled her straw around in her iced tea. "I thought I'd buy the already prepared chocolate chip cookie dough you only have to bake."

"Ah, what fun are you? I think we should take flour, and sugar, and... "

"Sam, it'll be so much easier with the already prepared dough."

"Okay," Samantha said with her lip turned down. "Party pooper." With her head bent down she looked up at Gillian, to see her reaction. And they both laughed.

"Remember, you're supposed to be the adult at camp, and not act like one of the kids." Gillian gave her the eagle eye.

"Oh Gilly. You really *are* a party pooper!" Samantha smiled.

Chapter Eighteen

Gillian parked, got, out and opened the trunk. Joining her, Samantha reached in and retrieved the dresses. "I'm going to take these upstairs and hang them up." Samantha said.

"Okay. I'm going to see if I can find a box for the tea party stuff."

Gillian searched the garage, but could only find either too small or too big of boxes.

Dusty strolled into the garage. "What are you looking for?"

"I'm trying to find something to pack dishes and stuff in for camp." She brushed some strands of hair from her face. "I can't find the size I need." She continued to search.

"I might have one upstairs. Come on up while I check."

She followed him to the apartment. "Is Josh home?"

"He's at the Suds and Fluff doing his laundry." He pushed open the door and stood to one side to let her enter first.

It was the first time she had been inside the apartment since Josh and Dusty had moved in, and she was surprised at how bare, yet how neat the apartment was with two bachelors living there.

"Have a seat. Do you want something to drink?" Dusty said.

"No thanks." She perched on the edge of the couch while Dusty went down the hall. "Sam and I had lunch at McDonalds."

Soon he returned with a medium sized box. "Will this work?"

"It's perfect!"

He sat next to her on the sofa. "You have to take your own dishes to camp?"

"It's for a tea party." She gushed. "Samantha and I are planning to have a tea party for our campers. We'll bake cookies and there's a picnic table beside our cabin." She rushed on, "I have a blue and white checked table cloth and a vase and flowers and today I found a tea set with a tea pot and six cups and saucers to match."

Without taking a breath, she went on, "We bought wedding gowns...actually Sam bought them. And she's going to donate her prom dresses to camp. And we'll get dressed up too. Oh! I almost forgot the best part. I got a dress with beaded teapots all over it."

Dusty listened as he twirled the end of her pony tail with his fingers. "Sounds lovely."

She playfully shoved him. "It's perfect. It's...like...it's...a God thing."

Dusty held her chin and kissed her. With her head resting on his shoulder and his arms around her, she felt comfortable and protected.

They broke their embrace when they heard a thud at the door.

Josh pushed open the door and plowed through with a laundry basket filled with folded clothes.

Gillian straightened. "Hi, Josh."

Josh set the basket down on the floor. "I need a wife."

"You do?" Gillian said.

"Yeah, to do my laundry," Josh said.

Gillian laughed. "You're a chauvinistic. I don't think you're going to find one in this day and age. Most of the women I know are career women and half of them have husbands who do the laundry."

"You're kidding!"

"It's true," Gillian said.

Josh came over to where they sat and tickled her. "Well then. I'll just have to find me an old fashioned girl like you."

"Don't, Josh. Stop," she cried half teasing.

After more squeals, Josh stopped and fell beside her.

Later she picked up the box. "I'd better go."

"Here. Let me help you," Dusty said.

Gillian glanced over her shoulder. "See ya, Josh."

"Later," Josh picked up the laundry basket and headed toward the bedroom.

Outside, on the landing, Gillian noticed wood scraps stacked neatly against the back of the garage. "Are you going to be using the wood for anything in particular?" she asked.

"No. Why?" Dusty asked.

"There's a woodworking center at camp and I know they can always use more wood."

"I'll get it ready for you to take." He held up the box he was carrying. "Where do you want this?"

"I'll put the stuff from my trunk in it and then add the rest from the house."

"Are you going to have room for everything you're taking to camp?"

"Pastor Mike is taking one of the church's vans to camp and he said he'd take anything we can't fit in my car."

Dusty followed her to her VW. He lifted the bags out and placed them inside the box. "I'll carry it to the house." He carried it on his shoulder and taking her hand, they walked to the house. Inside he set the box on the kitchen table.

Samantha came down the stairs. "Where have you been? I've been looking all over for you." Seeing Dusty she stopped. "Oh, hi Dusty."

"I was with Dusty. He found a box for me." Gillian put her purse on the table.

"See you later," Dusty said and left.

*****

Later, while Josh slouched on the sofa munching Doritos and watching baseball on TV, Dusty was intent on what he was doing at the kitchen table. Across the top of the sheet of paper he wrote, 'Birdhouse Instructions'. With a ruler and pencil he drew precise lines of a simple birdhouse. After he completed the drawing he wrote the instructions for the project.

On Monday morning Dusty headed for Home Depot and purchased everything he needed to make the kits. He also bought a jig saw to cut out the holes. He made a pattern, and his new saw buzzed as Dusty cut piece after piece.

The following day he was hard at work like a bee collecting pollen. At the end of the day he prepared individual kits by placing wood pieces, fasteners, and hardware into paper bags with handles. Each kit was complete, except for the instructions. He'd forgotten to stop at Kinko's and make copies of the instructions. He wiped his hands on his cutoffs and with the instruction sheet in hand he left the apartment.

Standing on Gillian's front porch, he raised his fist to knock, but hesitated as he listened to her play the piano. When the music ceased, he tapped on the door.

She opened the door.

"Do you have a copy machine?" he asked.

"Uh-huh."

"Can I use it?"

She opened the door wider. "Sure. It's in here."

She led the way. After turning on the machine, she took the paper from him. "How many do you need?"

"Twenty-five."

"What is it?"

"It's instructions for a birdhouse...for the kids at camp...for the woodworking center," he said.

"Is that what all the noise was?"

"Uh-huh," he said.

"Can I see?"

"Sure."

She took the papers from the machine, handed them to him, and followed him out to the garage.

Dusty squatted on the driveway next to the boxes filled with the bagged kits and Gillian knelt beside him. Opening one of the bags, he spread the contents on the driveway.

She nodded toward the two cardboard boxes filled with bags of supplies. "You made all of these for the kids at camp?"

"Do you think they'll like them?"

She threw her arms around his neck, knocking both of them off balance. Sprawled on the driveway, she laid on top of him. With his hand behind her head, he guided her down to his lips and kissed her. This time she kissed him back.

Chapter Nineteen

Josh knocked on the door of Gillian's cottage. Gillian opened the door and pulled him close to her. "Please stay after everyone leaves. I need to talk to you," she gushed.

Josh found an empty seat in the living room where everyone waited for the New Hope meeting to begin. He hadn't seen Gillian look this happy in a long time and his mind played out all the possibilities of why she wanted him to stay. During the meeting, he half listened as he thought of what she wanted to talk to him about.

While Gillian had never taken a turn at any of the meetings, tonight she shared, "Some of you know my parents abandoned me... and I know I still need to work through some things. What I want to say tonight is... I want to thank Josh. I'm here because of him. I'm an anorexic and I was in denial, but because of Josh and some other friends... well they didn't give up on me. It's because of them I'm here and working through the steps. And I think I'm doing pretty well. I'm eating like a normal person again and I've even put on some weight." She smiled. "I'm very grateful to Josh for not giving up on me even when I didn't make it easy for him." She caught his eyes. "Thanks, Josh."

Josh returned her smile. *Tonight may be the night I'll tell her how I feel about her. Not like the time in San Clemente ending in a fiasco before I could tell her I love her. Tonight's different. Tonight she's so happy. Maybe she feels the same way about me.*

While on the road, and at night alone in his motel room, he had rehearsed over and over again what he would say when the time was right. Now the time had come. He would tell her tonight.

Later, after everyone had shared and a closing prayer said, the group visited with one another and lingered over brownies. *Will they ever leave?*

He could hardly wait until the last person finally left.

"See you next week," Gillian said and closed the door behind the last one to leave the meeting.

"I didn't think they'd ever leave." She went to the kitchen and brought out a plate of brownies. Although she had served brownies at the meeting, she had held some back. "I made these especially for you. I know they're your favorite."

"Umm. You do know the way to my heart." His blue eyes sparkled.

"You want some coffee?"

"Got milk?"

She brought a tall glass of milk from the kitchen and joined him on the sofa. In all the years he'd known her, she had never looked more beautiful than she did now. There was a glow about her.

"What's up?" he asked with a mouth full of brownie.

"First of all, I want to thank you for introducing me to Dusty."

"The look on your face is thanks enough," he said. "He's doing a fantastic job on the house."

"Yes, he is, but it isn't the house I'm talking about. I think I'm falling in love with him."

"What?" He could not believe what she had just said. All evening he had fantasized about her professing her love for him, not Dusty.

"I said I think I'm falling in love with Dusty."

He picked up another brownie from the plate on the coffee table and quickly returned it. He'd lost his taste for them for the first time in his life.

"You always said you'd never marry someone who didn't believe in God the same way you do."

"I haven't forgotten. I'm not talking about marriage. It's just, well... you've always been there for me in the bad times and the good. You and Sam are my best friends and... I wanted to tell you how I feel. I guess I thought you'd be happy for me."

"Dusty's a great guy and all... but what do we know about him? I've only known him for a year. He doesn't work, yet he seems to have money." Josh ignored the dejected look on Gillian's face as he continued his litany. "I'll grant you he's doing a good job on the house, but anybody can paint."

She jumped to Dusty's defense. "He knows about electrical... and plumbing... and foundations. He's checked them all."

"Did you get a second opinion?"

"No. I didn't think I needed one."

"Other than surfing, what kind of a future is there?" Josh said.

"I thought Dusty was your friend."

"He is, but I'm your friend too. And I don't want you to get hurt."

The glow she'd had all evening had turned to a furrowed brow. "What makes you think Dusty will hurt me?"

He moved closer to her and took her in his arms. "All I want is your happiness. And I'm not sure Dusty will make you happy." He held her close and longed to tell her how he felt about her, but reconsidered. "Have you told Dusty how you feel?"

"No." She choked back a sob.

Josh reasoned. Maybe there was still hope. He'd tell her how he felt about her, but not now. The timing was all wrong. It was late and he was tired after a long week on the road. "I'm really beat... can we talk about this tomorrow?"

"Okay," she murmured.

He said goodnight to her and struggled up the stairs to the apartment. He was in no hurry to neither see nor talk to Dusty, and he was glad Dusty was asleep when he slipped into the bedroom. He quietly undressed and climbed into the twin bed with his thoughts. *I'll bid my time. Maybe Dusty will slip up. And if he doesn't become a Christian, Gillian will never consider marrying him. I'll have to show her I'm the one she can depend on. We share the same belief in God. I must tell her how I feel about her before it's too late, if it isn't already. I'm gone all week while Dusty is here with her.* He was reminded of the saying 'absences makes the heart grow fonder'. Yet in this situation, he felt it was more like the other cliché 'out of sight out of mind'.

It reminded him of when he was away at school and Gillian was out of sight and out of mind. He had concentrated on his education, didn't date much, and didn't keep in touch with Gillian. Now it was different -- seeing her every weekend, being with her again had stirred dormant emotions. Now the timing was right, if only he wasn't traveling during the week, he thought. *I've got to make a change.* He turned and faced the wall, away from where Dusty slept in the other twin bed a few feet from him.

The following morning, Josh jogged for several miles. He returned to the apartment and showered. Soon he knocked on Gillian's front door.

"'Morning, Josh," Gillian said cheerfully, holding a cup of tea. "Want a cup of coffee?"

"Yeah."

She set the steaming mug in front of him and joined him at the kitchen table.

"Do you remember the night we went to dinner in San Clemente?" he asked.

"I wasn't very nice to you. I'm sorry."

"I'd planned to tell you I love you."

She ruffled his reddish curls, still damp from the shower. "I know you love me, Joshy." She'd used Josh's mother's favorite name for him.

"You haven't called me that since third grade." He took a sip of coffee. "The look you had last night, the glow of happiness Dusty put on your face. I wanted it to be me who you fell in love with."

Gillian gathered her thoughts. She didn't want to hurt him. "I'll always love you, but..."

"Oh no, please no buts," Josh said, trying to lighten what he thought she was about to say.

"I'm not in love with you," she said. Those were the hardest words for her to say to him. "Someday you'll find someone who's in love with you, someone who deserves you. I don't want anything less for you."

He had halfway expected it, but had been in denial just like she had denied she had anorexia. The only way he could cope, and for both their sakes, he changed the subject. "You got any more of those brownies?"

"I put them in a baggie for you." She brought them to the table as Samantha descended the stairs sleepily. "Brownies! Now this is my kind of breakfast," Samantha said joining them at the table.

Chapter Twenty

The morning fog lifted as the church service came to a close. Under the trees, worshipers gathered around the serving tables where coffee urns and platters of donuts were spread on top of blue and white checked table cloths. Dusty, Gillian, and Samantha stood with others under the trees at the Little Chapel by the Sea. "Where's Josh?" Gillian asked.

"He's having Sunday dinner with his parents," Dusty said.

"Sounds like a day for family obligations," Samantha said. "My parents have planned a birthday party for my sister-in-law and I'm expected to be there." She popped a hunk of donut in her mouth and mumbled. "Come with me Gilly," she said. "You know you're always welcome."

"I've made plans to visit Mrs. Dodge. She's expecting me," Gillian said.

"What 'bout you Dusty?" Samantha said. "My mom's a killer cook."

"Nah. Thanks anyway," he said.

"Well, I'd better run. I'll see you two later." Samantha headed toward the parking lot.

Gillian was in no hurry. "What are you going to do?" she asked.

"Not sure." His hands in his pockets, Dusty looked down at the ground forlorn like one of her students who had been picked last to play on the kickball team.

"Do you want to go with me to visit my grandmother's friend? She lives in a nursing home."

He brightened. "Sure."

They finished their drinks and Dusty took her empty foam cup, and stuffing it inside his own, he pitched them into the nearby trash can.

"Two points," she said, smiling. "Why don't you leave your car here. I'll drive."

He held her hand and ushered her to her car.

"Do you have a problem with me driving?" she asked.

"Nah. I'm cool about controlling women."

Arriving at the nursing home they found Mrs. Dodge sitting in a wheel chair in the common room, listening to someone playing 40's tunes on the piano. Gillian walked up to her, and then bent and kissed her on her wrinkled cheek. "Mrs. Dodge, I want you to meet my friend, Dusty."

"It's nice to meet you." Dusty reached out and took her frail hand and held it gently.

"It's nice to meet you too young man." Looking at Gillian she said, "You know how to pick 'em, dear."

Gillian and Dusty smiled at each other.

"Dusty is who I told you about. He's doing the repairs and painting Gram's house," Gillian said.

"What?" Mrs. Dodge looked confused.

Gillian repeated what she had said only louder.

"How lovely. The house always looked like a show place when your grandparents were alive. Your grandfather had the yard looking like a park. It kind of went downhill after he died." Mrs. Dodge looked off in the distance as though she were seeing the house as it used to be. "It was a different time then -- an easier time. Mothers didn't work like they do now. Your grandmother and I spent our summers on the beach with our children -- watching them play. They were as brown as coconuts."

It wasn't the first time Gillian had heard Mrs. Dodge's stories. She'd heard many of the same things from her grandmother. Yet Gillian, and Dusty, let Mrs. Dodge reminisce during their visit.

"I'm feeling tired," Mrs. Dodge said. "It's time for my nap."

"I'll see you soon," Gillian said as she bent down to give her a hug.

Mrs. Dodge whispered in her ear, "He's a looker, dear."

Gillian smiled.

Mrs. Dodge reached out her arthritic, gnarled hand. "Thank you for coming young man. You be nice to her now, you hear."

"I will." Dusty held her hand.

When they returned to the church, the only car remaining in the parking lot was Dusty's Mustang. They sat in Gillian's VW, neither wanting to leave. They talked and talked and talked, comfortable together. Dusty leaned toward Gillian and with his palm on her cheek he gently, then passionately kissed her and she responded to his kiss.

"I love you," he said.

And she loved him. Yet the words wouldn't come. She held back from telling him what she longed to say.

*****

The following Sunday, Dusty sat in the pew with the rest of the congregation of the Little Chapel by the Sea listening to Pastor Mike as he spoke. "Are you a ho-hum Christian or an Extraordinary Christian?" Pastor Mike asked the congregation. He paused and then repeated the question, "Are you a ho-hum Christian or an Extraordinary Christian?"

Dusty let his mind wonder. *Gillian is an extraordinary Christian.*

He concentrated as Pastor Mike read from the Bible. "Our Scripture reading from God's Word today is Revelation 3:15 through 20. 'I know your works; you are neither cold nor hot. Would that you were cold or hot? So, because you are lukewarm, and neither cold nor hot, will I spew you out of my mouth. For you say, I am rich, I have prospered, and I need nothing; not knowing that you are wretched, pitiable, poor, blind and naked. Therefore I counsel you to buy from me gold refined by fire, that you may be rich, and white garments to clothe you and to keep the shame of your nakedness from being seen, and salve to anoint your eyes, that you may see. Those whom I love, I reprove and chasten; so be zealous and repent. Behold, I stand at the door and knock; if any one hears my voice and opens the door, I will come in to him and eat with him, and he with me.'"

He set his Bible on the pulpit and gazed out across those seated in front of him. "Some of you will probably shudder in your seats today, others of you probably should be shuddering. Are you on fire for Jesus? Is He your passion?" He shouted. "Do you have a burden for the lost?" He picked up his Bible and held it up. "Will you share God's love and forgiveness of sins with your loved ones? Your neighbors? The world? Will you be on fire for Jesus and save the lost? Or will you be a ho-hum Christian and go about your life not caring that others will burn in hell, because you are comfortable -- because you are lukewarm? God will spew you out of His mouth," he yelled.

Pastor Mike concluded by reciting a portion of Scripture he had read at the beginning, "'Behold, I stand at the door and knock; if any one hears my voice and opens the door, I will come in to him and eat with him, and he with me."

Dusty was reminded of a picture of Jesus knocking at a door in the Bible storybook his mother used to read to him. The congregation sang as Gillian accompanied them on the piano the familiar hymn; the same hymn Billy Graham had used in crusades all over the world. "Just as I am, without one plea But that Thy blood was shed for me. And that thou bidd'st me come to Thee, O Lamb of God, I come! I come!" Dusty was moved by the music and felt persuaded to move forward. He stepped into the center aisle and walked the narrow way to the front. At the altar, Pastor Mike reached out his hand and welcomed him.

Dusty knew as he stood before the altar with Pastor Mike he wasn't making his decision for Gillian, but for himself. He felt God calling him to step out in faith. Dusty longed to follow God's plan for his life as he had watched Gillian, Josh, and Samantha testify and live for God. *I want what they have.*

*****

Gillian always felt emotional when someone came forward to receive Christ as their Savior, but this time, she felt the same emotion even stronger than ever before, except for when she also walked the aisle to receive Christ as her savior.

In the evening, as they strolled, hand in hand, along the shore, Gillian and Dusty had something uniting them, their mutual faith in God.

"Dusty, I need to ask you a question, and I need you to be honest with me."

"Of course." He squeezed her hand.

"Did you go forward today because of me?"

"No." They stopped walking and he faced her, holding both of her hands in his own. "I'll admit in the beginning I went to church to see you. I know it wasn't a good reason to go, but it's true. I hope this doesn't hurt your feelings, but I love God more than I love you. I didn't think it could be possible. Today I felt something I've never felt before. It was like I finally got it. I not only know God loves me and died for my sins...and I will spend eternity with Him in Heaven, but I feel a peace I've never felt before. It's hard to explain."

"I know. It's a God thing." She squeezed his hand remembering God's promise in John 15:16. He chose Dusty. "This is the second best day of my life."

"What was the first?"

"My own salvation," she said.

Standing at the shoreline, he pulled her close to him and she felt his hard body against her.

"Gillian Grant, will you marry me?"

She looked up at him, and holding his face in her hands, she brought it down to her meet her own and kissed him full on the mouth. "Yes, Dusty, I'll marry you."

"Yahoo!" He picked her up and twirled her around and around. "Yahoo!"

"Do you think it's too soon?" he asked.

"No, I don't. I feel like I know everything I need to know about you."

He covered her mouth with his lips and their kiss went on and on as the water rolled over their feet. As each wave came to an end, Gillian felt it was a beginning for them.

"I know we are going to have a wonderful life together. I, also, know there could be some hard times, but with God we'll get through them."

"I feel the same way." She threw her arms around him. "Oh, Dusty, I love you so much."

B J Bassett

They strolled back to the house. Sitting on a chaise lounge on the patio, he wrapped his arms around her. "I want to get married right away."

"Me too, but I've got so much going on right now. I've got Royal Family Kids' Camp next week and when I get back from camp I've got to get my classroom ready for school and..."

"What about during your Christmas break?"

She was thoughtful. "I always dreamed of an outdoor wedding right here in Gram's yard," she said.

"You can't count on the weather in December," he said.

They cuddled as the sea air grew cooler and eventually they went inside and drank hot chocolate. "We don't have to make any definite plans tonight. We can talk about it when you get back from camp," Dusty said.

Later they lingered over saying goodnight, not wanting to leave each other.

Chapter Twenty-One

Every inch of Gillian's VW bug was packed with suitcases, sleeping bags, pillows, toiletries, and snacks. Josh and Dusty had helped them organize and stuff their things into the car. Dusty leaned into the driver's side of the car and kissed Gillian.

"I'll miss you too," she said.

"Not as much as I'm going to miss you." Dusty kissed her again.

Josh and Dusty stood in the driveway waving as Gillian and Samantha drove off.

Gillian and Samantha stuck their arms out the widows at the same time and called, "See you in a week."

While Josh folded clothes, Dusty sat at the kitchen table and wrote a letter to Gillian.

Dear Gillian,

You just left and I already miss you. I'll have to do something to keep myself busy and try to keep my mind active. Working with my hands doesn't keep me from thinking, so I think I'll try to do some studying. I didn't tell you before you left, but I've been studying in the evenings and plan to take the test for my contractor's license.

I hope the week goes quickly for my sake. You see, I'm selfish and want you all to myself. It will be soon enough when I'll have to share you with your students.

I don't think you have any idea how much I love you and am looking forward to our life together.

Love, Dusty

He folded the letter, put it in an envelope, and sealed it. He went to find Josh in the bedroom packing for the week. "I want to get this in the mail tonight. You want to go out for pizza later and I'll drop it at the post office?" He asked.

"Sure." Josh put some socks into his suitcase. "You mean you already wrote to her?"

"Yeah, man."

"You've got it bad." Josh laughed.

I'm sure it wasn't easy, but Josh seems resigned to the fact Gillian loves me and not him.

*****

On the long drive, Gillian and Samantha gabbed about everything. Gillian confided in Samantha. "Sam, I'm scared... I've lost the feeling in my fingers."

"Really!"

"There's something else... I haven't had a period in months."

"What?" Samantha gasped. "Are you pregnant?"

"No, silly. I thought you knew me better." Gillian said, grimacing. "If I was, it would be immaculate conception. Like the Holy Birth since Dusty and I haven't been intimate. We plan to wait until after we're married." Gillian adjusted the visor against the sun in her eyes. "Besides, I'm not worried about not having a period. I'm sure it'll eventually start, but it really scares me I don't have any feeling in my hands."

Samantha thought carefully before she spoke. "I've checked on the Internet and the loss of feeling in your hands and no periods are classic symptoms of anorexia."

"I've read about it too," Gillian said. "I know I have a problem, and... I think the New Hope meetings are helping. I've started eating meat, and bread again, even french fries."

"Yeah, I've noticed. It's a start. Maybe it'll take a while before the feeling in your hands returns." Samantha changed the serious mood. Lightheartedly she laughed. "When you get your period, I'll give you a period party."

"Thanks a lot."

"That's what friends are for." Samantha flipped her hair over her ear. "Seriously, Gilly, I think you should at least tell Dusty about not having your period. It's only right. Put yourself in his place. You know if the situation were reversed, you'd want him to tell you."

"I know...and I plan to tell him. I just need to find the right time."

After arriving at camp, Gillian and Samantha found their cabin and unpacked. Then they went to the mess hall to meet the rest of the staff. Later, before going to sleep, Gillian sat on her cot and wrote a letter to Dusty.

Dear Dusty,

We've spent the afternoon and evening of our first day getting ready for the campers. My campers' names are Lindsey and Kari, and Samantha's are Kendra and Shelby.

There is a door between our side of the cabin and the other side. We met the counselors on the other side today. This is their second year as counselors and they are very helpful.

We've decorated the cabin with tiny white lights and all kinds of things little girls like. Samantha has set up a mini beauty salon where the girls can put on makeup and we can give them manicures. We've got all kinds of things like tiaras and flowers they can put in their hair.

We've also decorated big colorful posters with the campers' names on them to welcome them when they get off the bus. I understand when the kids arrive on the bus tomorrow morning, it's really emotional for the staff. The day starts with treating these kids like royalty and continues throughout the week.

I'm so excited I probably won't be able to sleep tonight, but I know I have a tiring week ahead of me, so I've got to try to get some sleep.

Although we've only been apart for several hours, I miss you terribly. Do you think absence makes the heart grow fonder? I do.

I love you, Gilly

She planned to mail the letter first thing in the morning. She unplugged the little white lights and snuggled down into her sleeping bag, while Samantha put some finishing touches on the decorations.

On Wednesday, Gillian took a short break from her camp counselor duties and jotted a note to Dusty.

Dear Dusty,

Our days are very full with little time for ourselves, only a quick shower or a short walk for some respite. Today I decided to write to you during my break.

I hope you miss me as much as I miss you. I long to surf with you and, I know this sounds silly, smell you. You smell so good. And I can hardly wait to get home and see you and tell you about this life changing experience.

You would not believe what some of these kids have been through. They are so sweet. One camper is a seven-year-old brunette, with her front teeth missing who smiles all the time and is a joy to be with. My other camper is also seven, a towhead who never smiles. She is very sweet also.

Some of the kids are a handful, so I've been blessed with these two little girls.

Until I see you on Saturday, all my love,
Gilly

She addressed the envelope and jogged to the mess hall to get it in the mail before the carrier arrived. She returned to the cabin in time to take her campers to the dress up area to don prom dresses for the tea party.

Kari chose a slinky red dress, while Lindsey wore a ruffled pink net one. She twirled around. "Do you think I look like a princess, Gilly?" Lindsey asked.

Gillian wanted to see a princess, but no matter how magical the costumes were, she knew these kids came from horrible abuse. Parents were meant to be as sure as the rise and set of the sun, but some turned out to be monsters. She remembered her own parents, like cardboard facades. A lump caught in her throat. She met Lindsey's eyes. "You're a princess to me."

*****

On Saturday morning, Dusty busied himself by planting white daisies and pink geraniums around the house to fill in the areas which were trampled during painting. He bought two large ceramic flower pots for either side of the front door and planted pink geraniums in them. He planned to finish by noon so he could clean up for Gillian and Samantha's arrival. He sat upstairs in the apartment, gazing longingly out the window when the VW bug pulled onto the driveway. He jumped up and raced down the stairs. He grabbed Gillian and held her so tight, burying his nose in her hair.

"Hey, I went to camp too you know," Samantha said, getting out of the passenger side of the bug.

Dusty went over to Samantha and gave her a bear hug too.

"The place looks great." Gillian smelled the new flowers, touching the velvety petals.

Unable to contain himself he said, "I have a surprise for you." With his hand on the middle of her back, he guided her toward the house. "Close your eyes." Putting his hands on her shoulders, he guided her through the front door and into the living room with Samantha following them.

"Now you can open them," he said.

In awe, Gillian and Samantha gaped at the newly painted room. Dusty had painted the walls the color of coffee with lots of milk in it. He had added a decorative molding to the top of the walls and painted it white as well as the door frames. "Dusty, it's beautiful." Gillian turned around and threw her arms around his neck, and then she eyed the white daisies on the kitchen table. "You are good to me."

"I plan to be good to you for the rest of our lives," he said, with his arms around her waist.

They sat together in the living room, the excitement of their week at camp intoxicating. An hour passed as they described the children, caressing each description with love and hope as they vied for Dusty's attention, each with a favorite anecdote. Within moments they felt the physical and emotional drain descend imperceptibly until it weighed on each like a magnet's pull to the earth.

"I'm going to take a nap," Samantha said, and trudged up the stairs to her bedroom.

Lying on the sofa, her head in Dusty's lap, Gillian continued to talk. He stroked her hair, and within minutes she fell asleep.

Chapter Twenty-Two

The following week Dusty and Gillian were inseparable, except when Dusty studied for his contractor's license and Gillian prepared for her return to the classroom and a new batch of students. She planned to do some things the same way as before, things like hugging each child as he or she entered the classroom in the morning and again at the end of the day. Yet she wanted to bring new energy to her teaching. She held the list of new students in her hand as she prayed for each one. She longed to give each child what he or she needed -- whether it was improving reading skills, science discoveries, math skills, or her love. Her love was what some of them needed most of all.

Dusty tapped on the french door before opening it. "How about a burger for lunch?"

Gillian joined him in the living room, drying her hands with a dishtowel. "Not healthy, but why not."

They climbed into Dusty's Mustang and were soon sitting across from each other at In-N-Out.

Dusty reached across the table and, with a napkin, wiped mustard which had oozed from Gillian's burger and was at the corner of her mouth.

"Thanks."

"For what?" He stopped chomping.

"For taking care of me."

"I plan to take care of you for the rest of our lives."

Although she believed she would always be somewhat independent and more than likely Dusty would always let her be herself, she liked his plan to take care of her and love her. "I plan to take care of you too," she said.

He grinned. "It's a deal."

They lingered over their drinks. "My mother's birthday is Saturday and I plan to take off tomorrow morning to visit her." He reached across the table and held her hand. "Why don't you come with me?"

"It sounds tempting. And I'd love to meet her, but I feel responsible for the New Hope group. With Josh not coming home until Saturday this week, I especially need to be at the meeting tomorrow night. I don't feel right canceling it on such short notice."

"Could Sam do it?"

"She has a date."

"Oh yeah. With who?"

"Some guy from work."

His disappointment showed as he pulled his hand away.

"I'm sorry."

"It's okay," Dusty said. They left the restaurant holding hands.

*****

The next day after raising the flag together, Dusty drove along the coast on Highway 1 north to Santa Cruz. He slipped a new worship and praise CD, which Gillian had given him, into the player. It was a beautiful day for a drive and he was looking forward to seeing his mother.

Laura Bennett, a pert blonde, greeted Dusty on the wide front porch. She had recently quit her job as secretary for the law firm of Baker, Bennett, and Ross and married Matthew Bennett, one of her former bosses and a widower. With her flair for organization, she now devoted more time to charity work.

"I'd hoped you'd bring Gillian with you," she said, after receiving a bear hug from her son. "I so want to meet this girl who has captured your heart." With their arms around each other's waists, they entered the Bennett home. On the large marble floor foyer stood a round, cherry wood center table which held a vase of white lilies. An elegant winding staircase ascended to the second level. They skirted around the center table and stepped down into the sunken living room with lush white carpet and white brocade furniture, floor to ceiling windows on every side with a view of Santa Cruz.

She pulled Dusty down to sit next to her on the sofa. "Tell me all about Gillian," she said. "You call her Gilly, right?"

"I do." Dusty settled into the plush sofa. "I didn't think I'd ever find someone after Jennie."

Laura's sensitive expression reminded Dusty of the emotional and devastating time in his life. His mother had always been his anchor, especially during difficult times.

"At first I didn't like Gilly. Too serious and uptight. It was obvious she had an eating disorder. After a while, I got to know her for who she is. She's beautiful...on the outside and the inside too, like you, Mom, yet she's different. She has thick brunette hair...hazel eyes...a beautiful smile and an infectious laugh. She's strong yet vulnerable."

"Did you say she's a teacher?"

"She teaches fourth grade, and she plays the piano and teaches Sunday school too."

"I want to hear everything about your proposal and wedding plans, but first, would you like a drink?" She asked as she headed toward the kitchen.

"Just water."

"Not a beer?" Her eyebrows arched.

"I don't drink beer anymore."

"You don't?"

"It's important to Gilly, and since it's important to her, it's important to me too. I'm probably better for it."

"I'm impressed."

She returned and handed Dusty a tumbler of ice water. "Matt is having dinner at the club with his partners and clients tonight. I begged off. So how about taking your old mother out for dinner?"

"You're not old, Mom."

"Is Sanderlings okay?" she asked.

"Sounds good."

*****

Dusty had always been proud to be seen with his mother and tonight was no exception. In the restaurant, heads turned as Laura and Dusty strolled behind the maître d'. Laura wore a periwinkle linen sheath with a matching cropped jacket and her signature opera length pearls.

After ordering, Dusty looked across the table at his mother with the view of the surrounding manicured grounds and the Pacific behind her. "Mom, did you save your wedding dress from when you and Dad got married?"

"I did." She looked quizzically at Dusty. "Why?"

"I'm not sure if Gilly would want to wear it or not, but when I showed her your wedding picture, she commented on your beautiful dress."

"I haven't looked at it in years. It's stored in the attic. We can go up there tomorrow and see what condition it's in." She sipped ice water from the goblet.

During dinner, Dusty filled his mother in on the restoration of the beach house and his decision to obtain a contractor's license; mostly he talked about Gillian.

"I haven't seen you like this in a long time. You seem beyond happy," Laura said.

"There's a reason." He met her gaze. "I've become a Christian."

"I thought you always believed in God." She looked puzzled.

"I did, but now I have a personal relationship with Jesus, and it's partly because of Gilly." He placed his napkin on the table. "Mom, you're going to love her."

"I'm sure I will." She hesitated, then said, "Let's go home. I can't wait to find my wedding gown."

After parking his mother's Mercedes in the three-car garage, they walked up the lighted path to the front door.

Laura unlocked the door and they ascended the stairs. The unique attic was through a door in the master bedroom, like a huge walk-in closet. They entered the darkened cave and Laura fumbled for the light switch, only to discover the light bulb was burned out. "I'll go find a bulb downstairs," she said.

"Do you want me to go find one?"

"No. I know right where they are." She giggled. "Be back in a jiffy."

She returned with a bulb and a flashlight, giving them to Dusty. He moved around all sorts of treasures of yesteryear, found the socket and screwed it in.

"Voila," Laura said.

Dusty helped her remove boxes, stacked on the top of her hope chest. He remembered it was given to her by her parents when she graduated from high school. She opened the lid and a whiff of cedar filled their senses. She knelt in front of the treasure chest and took out a heap of Dusty's school papers.

She sat back on her haunches and handed half of the stack to Dusty to look at and the other half she put in her lap. There were pictures he had drawn of pumpkins, fish, and a rendering of the Santa Cruz Mission, from when he studied California history. There were math and English papers marked with big red "A's" and a report card representing each grade. In the comment section, teachers wrote things like "Dusty is a sweet boy," and "I wish I had a classroom full of Dustys."

"Did you save everything?" he asked, as he took out a box filled with neatly arranged Little League trophies. "I remember throwing this box of trophies in the trash years ago."

"I know."

"Did you get them out of the trash?" he asked incredulously.

"Yes."

He pulled out another box. Inside he discovered little plastic soldiers. Next a box of Legos was opened. The pieces were worn, some encrusted with a snack of peanut butter crackers. "Wow! I can't believe you saved all this stuff!"

She unfolded a little blue velveteen suit with a white shirt. Dusty had worn it for his first portrait taken when he was a year old. At the very bottom of the chest was the American flag, folded in the shape of a cocked hat, with the stars showing. Laura silently and lovingly placed her hand on top of the flag. Dusty was silent too, trying once again to imagine the father he never knew. Laura had filled his youth with stories about his dad. Her words were so vivid. Sometimes he felt he could see his dad.

Next to the flag was a large box tied with a ribbon. Laura lifted the box out of the chest and untied the ribbon.

"Laura? Dusty? Anybody home?" Matthew Bennett called.

Dusty went to the top of the stairs. "We're up here," he yelled.

A striking man in his fifties with premature grey hair wore a dark suit, his tie loosened and the top button of his shirt undone. In good physical condition, he took the stairs agilely. Reaching the landing, he put a firm hand on Dusty's shoulder and said, "How ya doing, Dusty?"

"Fine." They shook hands. "Mom's in the attic." They entered the master bedroom and both ducked to get through the small opening to the attic, where they joined Laura.

She had opened the box and was holding her wedding dress up, turning it from front to back and to front again, gazing at it when Dusty and Matthew came into the attic.

"It's in perfect condition. It hasn't yellowed, or anything," she said.

"Hi, honey," Matthew said, and leaning down kissed Laura on the cheek.

"How was dinner?" Laura carefully folded the dress and put it back into the box.

"It was okay. How was yours?" Matthew asked.

"It was great!" Laura smiled.

Dusty put all the things back into the cedar chest while Laura kept the wedding dress box out. "Mom, I still can't believe you saved all my stuff."

"They're my little boy's treasures." She was thoughtful. "You may want them for your own son someday."

Matthew yawned. "It's been a long day. I think I'll excuse myself and take a shower."

Laura carried the box with the wedding dress as they left the attic.

"I'm going to go get my duffle bag and hit the hay too," Dusty said.

Before Dusty left the room, Laura stood on her tip toes and kissed Dusty's cheek. "Good night son."

"Night, Mom. See you in the morning."

Chapter Twenty-Three

Gillian arranged foam cups, sugar, cream, spoons, and napkins on the table while the coffee brewed. A pot of hot water for tea and bottles of cold water were added. Everything was ready when Sam had left on her date.

The group visited as late comers straggled in. Pastor Mike approached Gillian. "Is Josh coming?"

"No. He's still out of town," Gillian said.

"Then I think we should get started," he said.

"Everyone, please take your seats," Pastor Mike announced.

Gillian sat quietly listening to other peoples' stories -- some she was able to relate to and others she was not. Amber Holloway, with her head down, spoke softly as she tearfully shared her horror of growing up at the hands of her drunken step-father's sexual abuse. Gillian said a silent prayer of thankfulness that she had never experienced such vile abuse, and determined to reach out to Amber in the future. She vowed to be more understanding, more caring.

Loud pounding interrupted the meeting. Gillian tiptoed to the door as Pastor Mike continued to pray.

Betsy and Steve Shoemaker, Gillian's mother and step-father, stood on the porch.

In shock, Gillian's thoughts darted around inside her mind like a bird trapped inside a house, trying to escape. *How long had it been since she'd seen her mother? Five years? Ten? She looks like she's aged at least twenty years since the last time I saw her. Why this sudden visit? Why now?*

"Well, aren't you going to invite us in?" Betsy Shoemaker slurred.

Speechless, Gillian opened the door wider for them to enter the living room. Everyone in the group, some with Bibles on their laps, focused on who had entered.

Without waiting for an introduction, Betsy forged ahead into the center of the room and announced, "I'm Betsy Shoemaker. Gillian's mother."

Most just stared, while Pastor Mike reached out his hand and said, "I'm Mike Richards, Gillian's pastor. It's nice to meet you, Mrs. Shoemaker."

"Just call me Betsy." She stumbled back to the front door where Steve Shoemaker and Gillian stood frozen.

Gillian said a silent prayer. *Dear God, please help me. Give me strength.*

"I've come to take possession of my house." Betsy straightened her shoulders and draped her arm around Gillian's shoulder.

Gillian was assaulted by the stale odor of booze, etched in her senses since childhood.

Like the long moment between climbing the roller coaster track and then taking a nose dive headlong to the earth, Gillian's childhood with a mother in love with whiskey returned. "Let's go into the den," Gillian said.

As she looped her arm through Gillian's, Betsy turned to the awestruck group. "Excuse us," she slurred. "Come on, Steve, unless you want to stay here with these Bible thumpers." She giggled as they strolled toward the den.

Gillian guided Betsy to the overstuffed chair while she motioned for Steve to sit on the loveseat. Gillian perched on the desk chair in front of the computer and swiveled around to face them. "Mother, Gram left the house to me," Gillian said, in a calming voice she used with the children in her classroom, yet she did not feel calm.

Betsy jumped to her feet. "She couldn't have. It wasn't hers to give. This house was left to me in my father's will." Betsy paced. "I saw the will. It said...the house was left to me when he died and I was to let my mother live here until her death. So this is my house."

The numbness Gillian had felt after her grandmother's death flowed over her. *Could this really be happening? Or is it just a nightmare and I'm going to wake up?*

Betsy stood and began pulling file drawers open haphazardly. "I'll find it." She slammed the top drawer and went to the next. "My mother never threw anything away. It's in this house somewhere, and I'm going to find it."

Gillian glimpsed at Steve, slumped on the loveseat in a stupor, as he watched Betsy. Unlike Betsy, he was a quiet drunk. "Steve?" Gillian pleaded, in hopes he would do something.

He shrugged his shoulders.

Betsy slammed another drawer.

Pastor Mike poked his head inside the room. "Anything I can do?"

"No," Gillian assured him, with more confidence than she felt.

"I don't like leaving you here."

"I'll be fine."

"Everyone else has left. I'll leave now too, unless--"

Gillian ushered him to the front door.

"You have my cell number." He patted her shoulder. "Don't hesitate to call me."

"Thank you." Then she closed the door behind him. She was functioning on auto pilot, and didn't know where the roller coaster ride was going to take her next.

She heard a thud in the den and went to investigate. Steve was trying to lift Betsy off the floor without success. Blood oozed from a gash on her forehead. "She hit the edge of the desk when she fell," Steve said.

"I'll go get a damp cloth and a Band-Aid." Gillian hurried to the medicine cabinet.

Returning to the den, Gillian blotted the cut, remembering the times during her childhood when she had taken care of her mother during other sharp turns on other roller coaster rides.

"Let's see if we can get her upstairs to bed," Gillian said.

Going upstairs with Steve on one side of her and Gillian on the other, Betsy mumbled incoherently. After Gillian and Steve put her to bed, he asked, "Whose room is this?"

"It's mine!" Gillian stood with her feet planted firmly on the carpet and her fists on her hips.

"Where will you sleep?"

"I'll bunk with my roommate. You can get your things and stay here tonight." She grabbed her pajamas from the drawer and dashed out of the room.

*****

Later, Gillian heard someone burst through the front door and race up the stairs. *Samantha must be home.* She sprang out of bed like a firefighter upon hearing the alarm. She opened the bedroom door and watched her back out of her room.

"So sorry, excuse me," Samantha apologized.

"I'm here. In your room," Gillian called to her.

Gillian sat on the edge of the bed, her tear stained face in her hands. Samantha threw her purse and car keys on her bed and sat next to Gillian. "Pastor Mike called me on my cell and told me what happened." She hugged Gillian. "I am so sorry."

"What about your date?"

"It's no big deal. Besides, what are friends for anyway." She made it a statement, not a question.

Gillian was reminded why she loved Sam so much.

"What did Pastor Mike say?" Gillian asked.

"He said your mother showed up drunk during the New Hope meeting. He didn't give me any details. What are they doing here?"

"My mother said this is her house and she plans to take possession of it. She said my grandfather left it to her in his will with a condition that my grandmother could live in it until her death."

"You've got to be kidding."

"I'm not." Gillian grabbed a tissue from the bedside table, dabbed at her moist swollen eyes and blew her nose.

Samantha rubbed Gillian's back and stared blankly at the carpet.

"My mother said she saw the will. It was years ago, before I was even born. She ransacked the den looking for it. The New Hope group couldn't get out fast enough. Oh, Sam it was a nightmare. She was cussing and yelling." Gillian buried her face in her hopeless hands. "I was so embarrassed."

"Does Dusty know?"

"He left for Santa Cruz to visit his mother this morning. I left him a message," Gillian said.

"You must have rights...isn't there something somewhere about possession is nine tenths of the law...something like that?"

"I don't know."

"Well, you'll have to get a lawyer and fight," Samantha said.

Feeling numb and spent, Gillian stared at the wadded tissue clinched in her hand. She wasn't sure she had any fight in her. *Why hasn't Dusty called?*

Chapter Twenty-Four

Thumping in the attic awakened Gillian. She looked at the clock on the bedside table. It was ten o'clock. Sam slept soundly in the twin bed next to her. Gillian got up, wrapped her bathrobe around herself, and went into the hallway to investigate. Opening the bedroom door, she was greeted by the pull-down ladder which led to the attic. She hadn't been up there in years.

She remembered the last time she was in the attic. It had been with Gram. Gram had shown her the cradle which had held three generations -- Gram, Betsy, and Gillian. There were love letters from her grandfather to her grandmother stored in a red heart-shaped box which Gram did not share with her. And there were letters written to Gram from her brother, when he was in Vietnam, all neatly tied in a yellow ribbon. Gillian's doll house stood in a corner of the attic. She had loved her doll house and had spent hours playing quietly with her imaginary family, a mother, a father, and two children. The mother who never yelled and the father came home from work every day. It was a perfect family. A thud from above brought Gillian back to reality.

She climbed the ladder and spied her mother rummaging around.

Later, a cup of tea sat on the kitchen table in front of Gillian while she talked to Dusty on the phone.

"Dusty, my mother came while New Hope was here. She was drunk."

"Is she gone now?"

"No."

Did he hear the lump in her throat and the tears in her voice?

"You mean she's still there?" he asked.

"Yes."

"I'm leaving right now. I'll be there as soon as I can."

"But it's your mother's birthday today." Gillian fingered the edge of the placemat.

"She'll understand. Gilly, hang in there. I'm on my way."

Betsy ran through the living room toward the kitchen waving a piece of paper over her head and yelling, "I found it!"

"I've got to go," Gillian said.

"I'm praying for you," he said.

"Thanks."

Betsy laid the official document on top of the placemat in front of Gillian, smoothing out the folds. "See. I told you there was a will," she said.

Gillian read the section her mother pointed at.

Samantha came into the kitchen. "What's all the yelling about?" She tucked a thatch of hair behind her ear.

"My mother found the will," Gillian said.

Gillian returned her attention toward her mother. "Did Gram know about the will?"

"I don't know if she did or not. It was written a long time ago...before you were even born," Betsy said.

"So she might not have even known about it," Gillian said, "maybe she thought the house was hers all along."

"Maybe she did. We never talked about it. I just always knew. It was between your grandfather and me. Your grandmother was never good at business...so I never discussed it with her. It said she could live in the house until her death. And she did. Now I'm taking possession of what's rightfully mine. After all, missy, I am the daughter, not you."

Gillian read the document again. "Mother, I'd like a copy of this," Gillian said more firmly than she felt.

"I'm not letting it out of my sight," Betsy said.

"I have a copy machine in the den. You can watch while I make a copy."

"Oh." Betsy snatched up the document and held it close to her body, acting paranoid one of them was going to take it from her. "Why should I let you make a copy?"

"Humor me." Gillian hoped her flippant attitude would work.

After making a copy, Gillian handed the original to her mother.

Betsy grabbed it and folded it, creasing the fold with her thumb and index finger. "I don't know what you think you can do about it. It's all legal," Betsy said, and left the room.

Feeling defeated, Gillian said, "She's right. It says the house is hers. There's nothing I can do about it."

"You're acting like a victim. And you said recently you'd never be a victim again," Samantha said, her hands on her hips. "Take control, Gillian, like you usually do."

Gillian sat a little taller in her chair. "I guess it wouldn't hurt to at least contact a lawyer." Her expression turned downtrodden again. "Who am I kidding? I can't afford an attorney."

"Did your grandmother have one?" Samantha asked.

"No, she never needed one," Gillian said.

It was silent as both women thought about the situation. After a while, Samantha broke the silence. "I don't know about you, but I can't stand being in the same house with her. She's crazy." Samantha quickly apologized. "I'm sorry, Gilly, I know she's your mother."

"It's okay. I feel the same way. Let's get out of here."

Gillian grabbed her purse, then they headed out the door together. "Sam, will you drive?"

"Sure."

Gillian tossed her car keys to Samantha.

They left in Gillian's yellow VW bug.

At Ruby's Diner in Balboa, Gillian drank a cup of hot tea and watched Samantha down an omelet. When they left Ruby's, they headed for the church in hopes of finding Pastor Mike.

Pastor Mike's car was the only one in the parking lot. He was in his office

Gillian tapped at his office door.

"Come in," he called.

"I'm sorry to bother you, Pastor Mike," Gillian said.

"You're not bothering me," he said. I was just going over last minute sermon preparation."

Gillian and Samantha sat in the matching burgundy leather chairs which faced the cluttered, massive cherry wood desk. Hundreds of books filled the floor to ceiling book cases surrounding Pastor Mike's office.

Pastor Mike leaned his tan arms on the desk and folded his hands. "Now, what can I do for you?" he asked. His clear blue eyes were full of compassion.

"For one thing, we want to get Gillian on the prayer chain," Samantha said.

"It's already been done..," he said. "In fact, the New Hope group came to the church last night after the meeting and prayed for you and your mother, Gillian." he said.

"Thank you," Gillian said. She felt the tears threatening.

"I want to thank you again for calling me last night." Samantha flipped her hair behind her ear.

"You're welcome," he said. He looked from Samantha to Gillian.

"Did you hear what happened last night?" Gillian asked.

"Only bits and pieces," he said. "Something about the house belonging to your mother...and something about a will."

Gillian scooted to the edge of the chair. "My mother found the will this morning and it is her house."

"Isn't there something about possession being nine tenths of the law, or something like that?" Samantha asked.

"I'm not a lawyer," he said, "but I think Ed Bower could help you." He rummaged around on his desk and came up with the church phone directory. "He's a church elder and the church's attorney."

"I know Mr. Bower. I have his granddaughter, Emma, in my Sunday school class," Gillian said. "I guess I could call him and at least see what he charges."

Gillian and Samantha stood and Gillian reached out her hand. "Thank you, Pastor Mike. I appreciate what you've done."

"May God bless you." He stood and firmly held Gillian's delicate hand between his strong reassuring hands.

Gillian and Samantha said their goodbyes and left.

*****

Dusty took the stairs two at a time. "Mom. Mom."

Laura Bennett opened her bedroom door, her blonde hair wrapped in a towel like a turban. She wore a red embroidered Japanese kimono. "What is it?"

"I have to leave. Gillian needs me."

"What's wrong?" She followed him into the guest room.

"It's a long story." He stuffed his things into his duffle bag. "Her mother is causing a problem right now." He pulled out the little blue velvet box which held the pearl stud earrings and handed it to her. "Happy birthday, Mom. I'll call you later." He kissed her on the cheek and ran down the stairs. Dusty's Mustang sped around the curves on Pacific Coast Highway along the coast at Big Sur. It was a beautiful day with a smattering of white fluffy clouds in the blue sky. He was aware of the law about not using cellphones while driving, but this was an emergency. It was the only way to communicate with Gillian until he could get to her. He could stop and call her, but he wasn't willing to take any more time than necessary to make the long drive and be with her. He hoped God would forgive him for breaking the law. He punched the first number on his cell phone, Gillian's number.

"Hi," she answered.

"How ya doing?"

"I'm okay."

"Is she still there?" he asked.

"Yes."

"Why is she there?"

"She says this is her house," Gillian said.

"What?" With one hand on the steering wheel, he maneuvered the next curve effortlessly.

"She found my grandfather's will in the attic. She said she saw it once and it said the house was left to her."

"I thought it was your grandmother's house."

"I did too."

He had the feeling she needed to let it all out; he didn't say anything or ask any questions. He just listened, letting her vent.

After talking to Gillian and assuring her he was on his way, Dusty felt he had left his mother abruptly, and he felt strongly that he wanted to call her and explain. Laura Bennett answered the phone pleasantly and professionally like she had for all those years as the secretary of Baker, Bennett, and Ross.

"Mom, it's me. I'm sorry I left so abruptly without explaining."

"You said Gillian needed you. It's all I needed to know."

"Thanks, Mom." He turned down the volume on the CD player. "Gillian had a tough childhood. Her dad abandoned her when she was a toddler and her mother has a problem with alcohol and has also abandoned her for years at a time, only to come back from time to time and then leave again."

"The poor dear."

"Gilly's grandmother raised her and she died recently... Gillian thought her grandmother's house was left to her. It's the house I've been fixing up for her."

"Uh-huh."

"Well, her mother showed up after years of being gone and said there is a will and the house belongs to her." Dusty remembered the flag rising and got a new sense of the importance of it for Gillian. It wasn't just a house to her. It represented Gram and every pleasant childhood memory Gillian held.

"I understand why you rushed away. Son, you made the right choice to go to her during this crisis. I'm very proud of you."

"You get the credit, Mom. I'm just doing what I learned from you." His gas gauge arrow pointed below "E", so he pulled off the highway and looked for a gas station. "Mom, I feel badly about leaving you on your birthday."

"Don't give it a second thought. I'll have lots more birthdays."

"I got to go, Mom." He pulled into a 76 station.

"Bye, I love you."

"I love you too, Mom." He clapped his cell phone shut, slipped from behind the steering wheel, and filled his gas tank.

He tried over and over again to call Gillian with no response. He became more and more frustrated as the miles clicked away, his thoughts playing cartwheels in his head. After a while, he remembered the Bible verse he had recently memorized and repeated the words,

"With God, all things are possible." At San Luis Obispo he took the 101 Freeway, to make better time.

He tried to call Gillian several more times without success. He punched in Josh's number on his cell phone.

"Hi, Dusty, where are you?" Josh asked.

"I'm on my way home," he said, curtly. "Have you seen Gillian?"

"No...but there's a strange car in the driveway."

"It's probably her mother's car."

"What? Her mother's here?" Josh asked.

"Yeah. It's a long story."

Dusty heard loud thumping. *Was Josh going down the stairs?*

"Her car isn't in the garage. I'll check the house."

Dusty listened to knocking. "Hello, Mrs. Shoemaker. I'm Josh. Gillian's friend. Do you remember me?"

"I guess. You the little redheaded kid?"

"I live in the apartment." He cleared his throat. "Is Gillian here?"

"Nope."

"Her boyfriend's trying to contact her."

"I don't know where she is."

"Well, thank you."

"Whatever."

The door slammed.

Josh's voice came over the cell. "Did you hear?"

"Yeah. I heard. Thanks for trying, Josh. I owe ya."

Dusty pitched his cell phone into the passenger seat and prayed. "Dear God, please be with Gillian right now. May she feel your presence, I pray. Amen." He felt God's peace and knew with God's help, they would get through this together. He pressed his foot down on the accelerator.

Chapter Twenty-Five

The yellow VW bug zoomed along Cliff Drive. Before they reached the driveway, Gillian and Samantha saw the sign stuck in the ivy bank. As they got closer they could make out the words -- FOR SALE and below it, in smaller letters, By Owner.

"I don't believe it!" Samantha exclaimed.

"I can." Gillian shielded the sun from her eyes with her hand as Samantha pulled the car into the garage. "This is a prime piece of property. It's probably worth over a million. I'm sure she never wanted the house, only the money." Gillian got out of the car and slammed the door.

Samantha followed Gillian, who went straight through the house and onto the patio where her mother and Steve reclined on chairs watching the beautiful Pacific, each holding a can of Budweiser.

"I guess you saw the for sale sign." Betsy kissed the beer can, as she took a long draw on it.

"Yeah." Gillian felt numb.

Steve was silent as he nursed his beer.

With Samantha at her side, Gillian felt the disgusted look on her face must mirror her own.

"I don't want the house. I never did. It's worth big bucks, and since I'm only interested in the money, it's perfect. So as soon as it sells, we'll be out of here." Betsy drained her beer and got up. "Come on Steve. I want to go to the bar."

Steve followed behind Betsy like a faithful puppy as she left the patio. Gillian thought, *I wonder if he even has a mind of his own, or maybe he loves her, in his dysfunctional way.*

Gillian realized her mother was as different from her as rock music was to Brahms. She went inside, grabbed her recharged cell phone, and called Dusty as she returned to the patio and plopped down on the chaise lounge her mother had vacated. Samantha took the other reclining chair, her expression had turned from disgust to concern.

*****

Dusty had made the long drive in record time. As he drove up Cliff Drive, he swerved to miss hitting a clunker coming at him over the center line. He pulled up the driveway at the beach house in Reagan Beach just as his cell phone signaled Gillian was calling him.

"Hi," he said, "I've been trying to call you for hours."

"I'm sorry. Samantha and I've been gone all day," Gillian apologized. "We went to a movie and I turned off my cell."

"Where are you now?"

"Home." Her voice broke.

He parked, knocked on the front door and, when there was no answer, he entered. Seeing them on the patio he walked through the house and joined them. Gillian stood and fell into his arms, sobbing. After a while, he guided her to sit on the chaise lounge and together they sat side by side, facing Samantha.

"Did you see the for sale sign?" Gillian asked.

Dusty felt her tense muscles. "Yeah."

"Maybe it won't sell," Gillian rationalized.

"Does it really make any difference if she owns it or someone else does?" Samantha said.

Gillian tried to think straight. "I guess it doesn't matter. I just can't believe this is happening." She looked at Dusty. "You did so much work... and it looks so beautiful..."

Dusty was silent, yet his eyes said everything -- his love, concern, compassion.

Soon Josh came around the corner of the house. "I've been all over town looking for you two," he admonished, then quickly recanted, "I see everyone's okay."

"Yes and no," Dusty said.

"I saw the sign." Josh sunk into a patio chair. "What's going on?"

"Samantha and I will have to move," Gillian said. "I don't know about the apartment...if the rent will be raised or not...or even if you can still live there. My mother is the legal owner of the house," Gillian said.

"Bummer," Josh said, slumping in the chair.

*****

Surrounded by her friends, Gillian reached in her pocket and pulled out the copy of the will. She silently read the date the document was written and gasped. "My mother was only seventeen when my grandfather wrote his will. When he was alive, my mother was a very different person than she is now. Gram told me." She gazed into Dusty's eyes. "Gram said when he died, she was consumed with grief and couldn't do anything. It was my mother who taught her how to drive, pay bills, everything." Gillian felt like a spark plug had ignited. "It makes perfect sense to me now why he'd leave the house to my mother. He knew she'd take care of Gram. At the time he wrote the will, he didn't know the destructive road my mother would take."

Gillian was thoughtful, remembering more about her mother, things Gram had confided in her. "My mother never drank when my grandfather was alive. It wasn't until she went away to college and started hanging around with the wrong crowd. She eventually dropped out of school, met my father, and had me." Gillian dug deeper into her memory. "I know my grandfather spoiled her and she adored him. Maybe the alcohol numbs her pain." Gillian relaxed, feeling a sense of comprehension. "My grandmother probably didn't even know there was a will."

"So, what can you do about it?" Samantha asked.

"We'll figure something out," Dusty said. His arms tightened protectively around Gillian.

A gloomy silence hung in the air and was eventually interrupted. "Anyone want something to eat?" Josh asked.

"I'm not hungry," Gillian said.

"Me neither," Dusty said.

"I am. I'm gonna go get something to eat," Josh said, standing.

"I'll go with you," Samantha said jumping up. "Josh, since I'm going to be homeless, can I move in with you?" Before Josh could respond, Samantha added, "Just kidding."

As the sun set Gillian lay in Dusty's arms. "God works in mysterious ways."

"What do you mean?"

"The offertory I'm playing tomorrow is 'Because He Lives'" Knowing Dusty would probably not know the words to the hymn, she recited the chorus softly, "Because He lives I can face tomorrow. Because He lives all fear is gone. Because I know He holds the future. And life is worth the living -- just because he lives."

"How apropos," he said.

Soon they feel asleep on the recliner and never heard Samantha come home.

Chapter Twenty-Six

Gillian felt the warmth of the sun the following morning as she lay in Dusty's arms. Sleepily, she stirred and turned to face him. "We slept here all night!" she said.

He grinned through sleepy eyes. "Don't tell anyone we slept together."

She shoved him playfully. "I'd better get ready for Sunday school."

"I'll go with you."

"Really?"

"Really." He yawned and ran his hand through his hair. "What time do we leave?"

"I like to leave by eight thirty."

"I'll meet you at the car."

Dusty sat in a kid-size chair, his new Bible balanced on one thigh. He wore the same white silk shirt he'd worn on their first date. Libby Murdock sat close to him. Gillian observed the little girl gazing admiringly up at him.

Dusty helped the children build birdhouses. Gillian thought, *he's in his element, building, and he was so diligent during the week, gathering all the wood scraps for the project.*

"Is he your husband?" Libby Murdock asked.

Gillian looked down into her big brown eyes. "Not yet. Soon," she said, looking over at Dusty. She saw a new side to Dusty, being with the children.

After church, they grabbed some sandwiches and drinks and headed for Mason Park. Dusty spread a blanket under a tree and soon they plopped down and began munching Classic Combo sandwiches.

"What was the hymn we sang?" he asked.

"Do you mean 'Because He Lives'?"

"Right. It seems fitting...for what you're going through."

"I know." Nibbling on potato chips, Gillian was thoughtful. "I know I can't bury my head in the sand any longer. I'll have to think of this whole thing as a closed chapter in my life."

"I know how much you love the house." His compassionate eyes spoke more than his words.

Tears threatened as she swallowed a sob. "You worked so hard on it. And..."

She fingered the blanket. "And, if it's possible, I think you love the house as much as I do."

"It was a labor of love for both of us. And I think it was the catalyst that brought us together. Maybe, in a way, your grandmother had something to do with us meeting."

"I think she did too."

"Someday I'm going to build a house for you. If you want, I'll build one just like your grandmother's."

She lunged at him, throwing him off balance, and toppled on top of him. She wrapped her arms around him and planted a kiss on his lips. "Oh, Dusty, I do love you." But, in her heart, she knew another house could never take the place of Gram's house.

She sat up, and although she felt like she was on an emotional rollercoaster on the inside, she smiled. "There's a lot to do. I have a classroom to get ready for school...and we have a wedding to plan."

"Have you scheduled the church?"

"No..."

"You sound hesitant. You're not getting cold feet are you?"

"No... it's just I..."

"What?"

"Since I was a little girl, I've dreamed of an outdoor wedding at Gram's house," she said melancholy. "It's so beautiful with all the landscaping you've done. The lawn has never looked greener... and all the flowers."

"We can be married there," Dusty said.

"How can we if the house sells?"

"We'll push the wedding up."

"There's so much to do."

"We can do it! We restored a whole house in a few months. We can plan a wedding in a few weeks! I'll even help you get your classroom ready too."

"It'd be like a shotgun wedding."

He laughed. "Isn't a shotgun wedding for someone who's pregnant?"

"I don't know, I guess."

"Then it would be like a virgin birth, right!"

They laughed as Dusty tickled her and she pleaded, "Stop," in between giggles.

The following week, the "For Sale" sign was gone along with her mother and step-father. A note was left on the kitchenette table.

Gillian,

The house sold. The new owner will let you know when you need to move.

You'll be fine. You're not like me. You're like your grandmother. I couldn't live up to what she wanted me to be.

I'm sorry I wasn't the mother you needed.

I wish you well.

Mother

Gillian laid the note in her lap and let the tears flow unchecked. They streamed down her cheeks, she let all the tears out...the ones she had held for months and years while she tried to be strong and responsible, all the years of denying her life wasn't fine.

She sat up, wiped the tears away with her fingertips, went to the sink, and washed her face with cool water. "No more," she said, "I will never be a victim again."

Chapter Twenty-Seven

Samantha burst through the door carrying a huge box. "Gilly! Gilly!" She called.

Gillian came out of the den. "What is it?"

"Look! It's addressed to you." Samantha handed her the package. "I met the UPS guy out front. He's sooooooo cute."

"Right." Gillian gave her a knowing look.

"Well, he is!" Samantha said. "Open! Open already!"

Gillian sat on the sofa, juggling the box on her lap while Samantha dashed into the kitchen and returned with scissors. "Thanks," Gillian said as she cut the packaging top and lifted the lid. Inside, carefully wrapped in tissue paper was a wedding dress. Gillian recognized it from Dusty's photo. It was his mother's wedding gown. On top was a note. She unfolded it and read:

Dear Gillian,

When I spoke with Dusty, he said you hadn't found a wedding dress. If you still haven't found one and would like to wear mine, it is enclosed. I've had it cleaned, but it may need some alterations. The decision is yours and there will never be any hard feelings if you choose not to wear it.

I look forward to meeting you and welcoming you into our family soon.

Laura

Gillian stood and let the box fall to the floor as she carefully held up the beautiful white lace Victorian styled wedding dress.

"It's beautiful!" Samantha gushed. "Try it on."

Gillian rushed into the den and came out wearing the size six gown. "I think it'll only need a slight alteration here." She pinched together the side seams on either side of her waistline.

"Do you like it?" Samantha asked.

"I love it."

"You'd be nuts if you didn't."

Through the front window they spotted Dusty coming toward the house. "Quick! Hide! Don't let him see you." Samantha inched to the door as Gillian dashed into the den. "I'll get rid of him," Samantha called over her shoulder.

Opening the door a crack, Samantha acted cool. "Oh, Dusty, it's you."

"Yes. I live here you know."

"I know."

"Is Gillian here?"

"Uh. Well... she's indisposed... at the moment," Samantha stammered, flipping her hair behind her ear.

A muffled giggle came from behind the den door causing Samantha to smother her own laughter which was about to erupt. "Sorry. Come back later." Samantha succumbed to a fit of laughter.

"Okay, I'll go along with whatever game you're playing." He peeked inside the doorway. "I can hear you Gilly." Dusty grinned, than ambled away.

After he left, Gillian and Samantha sat on the sofa in the living room. Gillian held a tablet in one hand and a poised pencil in the other. Across the top of the tablet she wrote, "Things to do for Wedding."

"Dusty said he'd make sure the yard looks beautiful for the wedding. He plans to add a few more flowers. So I don't have to worry about the yard." She put a check mark beside yard.

Next she wrote the word reception and put a check mark beside it. "The ladies at church have organized the food and they plan to serve and clean up too," Gillian said.

"They're such Marthas," Samantha said.

"So the yard and the reception are taken care of."

Samantha interjected, "You have your wedding gown and I have my dress." Samantha tucked her feet under her. "Who's going to walk you down the aisle?"

"I've considered Pastor Mike... or maybe Josh."

"Josh would love it." Samantha beamed. "Actually, either one of them would probably consider it a privilege."

"I haven't decided for sure. Dusty asked Josh to be his best man. I guess he could do both." Gillian shrugged her shoulders. "I may just walk down the aisle alone." Gillian scanned the 'To Do List', then placed it in her lap.

Samantha checked her watch. "Gilly, I got to run. I'm late for my manicure." She jumped up. "Just let me know what you need me to do. Okay?"

"Sure."

Alone in the house, Gillian made herself comfortable in the overstuffed floral chair beside the living room window overlooking the Pacific. She tucked her legs under her and put pen to paper.

Dear Mother,

Although you will never read this letter, I need to write it for my sake. Now I know I need to love you unconditionally like God loves me.

I don't really know what happened in your life for you to make the choices you've made. Maybe Grandpa was too lenient with you. Maybe you got mixed up with the wrong crowd when you were young. I don't know, and it really doesn't make any difference.

I'm writing this letter to you to hopefully help heal my past hurts.

I forgive you for abandoning me. I was blessed to have Gram and I thank you for that. I also forgive you for all the times when I had to be the adult because you were the child. I believe I am the person I am today by God's grace.

I do not wish you harm. It is my prayer that someday you will soften your heart to the nudge of the Holy Spirit and find the personal relationship and abundant life you can only have by accepting God's free gift of his only Son, Jesus.

In some ways, I wish I knew where to mail this letter and that you would read it in the spirit it is written. And you would accept God's free gift of Jesus with open arms.

With my prayers and love,
Gillian

After signing the letter, she thought about putting it in her Bible, but thought better of it. She did not want to be reminded of it every time she opened her Bible. It was a closed chapter in her life and she chose to move forward. She strolled to the den, took a blank file folder, and wrote 'Mother' across the top. After she slipped the letter inside the folder, she placed it, in alphabetical order, in the file cabinet. She closed the drawer and strolled outside. First she sighed heavily, then she took a deep breath, breathing in the fresh sea air. Ambling over to the rose garden, she bent and nuzzled a perfect yellow rose. The fragrance filled her senses. "Gram, I know I'm going to miss this place... but I also know wherever I am, you'll be with me." Catching sight of the bench Dusty had bought for the rose garden brought a smile to her. She sat down and ran her hand over the smooth surface. "Gram, you'd love Dusty. He's not only handsome, but he's everything and more than I could have ever dreamed." She sat for a long time peacefully remembering.

Chapter Twenty-Eight

Gillian watched as Laura Bennett stepped off the plane at John Wayne Airport into a throng of passengers -- tourists visiting Disneyland, Knott's Berry Farm, the Southern California beaches, and those who came to meet passengers. Dusty held up his hand and waved. "Mom, over here."

Wearing a beige linen pant suit with a blousy jacket and a pink silk shirt accessorized with gold jewelry, she moved through the crowd toward Dusty and Gillian. Dusty greeted Laura first with a warm embrace. "This is Gillian."

Gillian handed Laura the bouquet of white daisies she had picked just before driving to the airport. "It's so nice to meet you."

"It's delightful to meet you, Gillian." Laura hugged Gillian with one arm and took the flowers in her other hand. "They're lovely. Thank you," she said, glancing down at the bouquet and admiring the flowers. "I appreciate your thoughtfulness."

After Dusty retrieved the luggage, Laura asked, "Where are the car rentals?"

"We have two cars, I'm sure you don't need to rent one."

"Please indulge me. I'd rather not inconvenience anyone. With the wedding only a week away, there'll be a lot to do and three cars will be better than two," Laura said.

"I can see you've made up your mind." Dusty led the way.

They arrived at the Enterprise rent-a-car counter where Laura completed the necessary paperwork. Dusty stowed her luggage in the trunk and they were soon on their way.

"You can follow me."

"Gillian, will you ride with me? In case I lose Dusty."

"Sure," Gillian said, and slid into the passenger seat of the rented Cadillac.

Laura put on her oversized Gucci sunglasses and followed Dusty's Mustang out of the airport parking and into the southern California traffic. "I want you to know how much I appreciate the opportunity to spend this week before the wedding with you and Dusty."

She expertly followed Dusty's Mustang onto the driveway and parked behind it. "What a lovely place." Laura exited the car and shut the door.

"Let's go around to the back so you can see where the wedding ceremony will be held." Gillian led the way, passing white daisies and pink geraniums in abundance. As they strolled under the arched trellis covered with baby pink roses, then continued along the used brick path. "Dusty did all the brickwork. He redid the patio," Gillian said proudly.

Reaching the lush green lawn and the rose garden overlooking the Pacific, Laura marveled at the beautiful setting. "This looks like *Better Homes and Gardens* or *Brides* magazine."

Working together, they had undertaken the needed repairs and beatification of the Cape Cod cottage, resulting in a restored showplace of what the original must have looked like. Gillian knew it took more than hard work to accomplish what they did. It was tender loving care.

Gillian opened the french doors off the patio and ushered Laura inside. "Dusty painted the living room while I was at camp."

"Beautiful. It's a lovely home," Laura said.

"Thank you." Gillian kept her fear in check of losing the house she and Dusty had worked diligently to restore. A labor of love which had begun as a tribute to her grandmother and now was something they had created together only to be lost to them. If she let herself, she knew she would cry, so she shook off the dark mood as best she could. "Would you like something to drink?"

"I understand you like tea?" Laura said.

"Earl Grey's my favorite," Gillian said.

"I'll have a cup of tea."

Laura and Dusty sat at the kitchen table as Gillian prepared the tea.

"Dusty, you want something to drink?" Gillian asked.

"No thanks, I only drink tea when you wear the teapot dress." He leaned back in the chair and grinned.

"What's this about a teapot dress?" Laura asked.

"Gillian found this dress with teapots on it at the thrift store. She wore it at Royal Family Kid's Camp and had tea parties for her campers."

Laura laughed. "What fun they must have had."

"It was fun." Gillian smiled

"It's a wonderful thing you did for those children being a counselor at camp," Laura said.

"The purpose of the camp is to give the campers a week of happy memories, but I think I was as blessed as they were -- or more." Gillian took her grandmother's delicate tea cups from the cupboard and placed them on the table.

"If I remember correctly, Dusty said the camp is for foster kids."

"That's right." Gillian put two Earl Grey tea bags in Gram's favorite teapot with all the tiny lavender flowers on it. "My best friend and roommate Samantha and I were counselors for four sweet little seven-year-old girls." She poured the boiling water into the teapot and brought it to the table.

"I'm sure you and your friend accomplished the purpose of the camp and gave those little girls happy memories." Laura accepted the cup of tea Gillian offered.

"I know she did!" Dusty said proudly.

"Dusty, I brought the sand you asked for, but I still don't understand what it's for," Laura said, with a confused look on her face.

"You've seen the lighting of the Unity candle at weddings?" Dusty said. "We've decided to do something like it only with sand."

Gillian added, "I saw it at a friend's wedding recently. Both Dusty and I love the beach. So we decided I would pour sand from here and Dusty wanted the black sand from Santa Cruz to represent him. During the ceremony, we will pour it into a clear container, and together the grains of sand become one. The Unity Candle's flame will go out, but the Unity Sand will be displayed in a special place in our home as a memory of our wedding day."

Gillian went to the den and came back to the sofa carrying a box with the three clear glass containers inside. She pulled out one, which looked like a tall iced tea glass, and showed it to Laura.

"What a unique idea." Laura reached into her purse and pulled out the keys to the rental car. "Dusty, the sand is in my overnight case. Why don't you bring in my carryall? It has the photo albums you asked me to bring too." Laura handed the keys to Dusty.

"Thanks, Mom. I'll be right back"

While Dusty retrieved the bag, Laura continued. "What a darling idea to put together a video of you and Dusty growing up and show it at the reception. I had so much fun looking at the pictures, but I didn't pick out any to use. I thought you and Dusty would like to do it."

"I'll go get the pictures I've chosen," Gillian said. She returned the Unity Sand containers to the den and brought back the photos she had chosen of herself for the video. She nestled on the sofa next to Laura. "These are the ones I've chosen of me for the video." She showed Laura a couple of photos with her grandmother, but most of them were of Gillian alone -- a couple baby photos, first day of school holding a Winnie the Pooh lunch pail, one in her cheerleading uniform, and one with her church youth group.

Dusty returned with the bag and Laura took out the albums and put them in Gillian's lap.

"We'd better decide which ones we want to use of Dusty now and take them to the video place tomorrow. The guy told me he'd do a rush job for me," Gillian said.

Laura and Dusty sat on either side of Gillian as she turned the pages. Dusty pointed to a photo of himself at eighteen months wearing diapers and sniffing a rose in the garden. "Please not that one," he pleaded. "I look like I have a load in my diaper."

"I think it's cute," Gillian said.

"So do I," Laura agreed.

They flipped through the pages and selected ones of Dusty as a baby, a toddler, some with Dusty and Laura, and some with Dusty and Pop. Also, Little League photos, Dusty in a school military uniform, high school graduation, and lots of surfing photos throughout his life. Gillian was pleased with how she imagined the video would turn out -- matching up with her own photos of important events and people in her life. Gillian said, "I just realized we don't have any pictures of us together. We've been so busy and everything has happened so fast, we haven't taken any pictures of us together."

Laura reached in her purse and pulled out her digital camera. "There's no time like the present."

They went outside and as they posed on the cliff with the horizon behind them, Laura clicked. "Now, over here," Laura said, guiding them to the rose garden. "What about some under the rose covered archway?"

Laura continued to snap pictures. There were shots of them holding hands looking into each other's eyes, some of Gillian in front of Dusty, his arms clasped around her. Some of them standing and some sitting on the new bench Dusty had bought at Home Depot on one of his trips. He had surprised Gillian with it. There was even one of Gillian sitting on the bench with Dusty holding her hand and kneeling on one knee. "Now, let's see how they look." Laura handed the camera to Gillian. "You should be able to use some of these."

Laura covered her mouth with her hand to stifle a yawn. "Excuse me," she said, "I think I'd better call it a night."

"My room is...ready for you," Gillian said. "I'm bunking with Sam tonight."

"Thank you, but I plan to stay at a hotel."

"We thought you'd be staying with us," Dusty said.

"I've already decided." Laura took Gillian's hands and held them between her own. "Preparing for a wedding can be stressful, and I want to do whatever I can to help make it a time of joy. Besides, I need my privacy. Dusty can tell you I love people, but I also love my alone time too." She winked at Dusty. "Right, son?"

"Right Mom."

"I'll be staying at the Marriott." Laura wrote the hotel information on a piece of paper. "My cell phone is still the best way to contact me.

"I have something to wear to the wedding, but I'd hoped you could spare me some time for a mother-in-law and daughter-in-law shopping trip." Laura's eyes caught and held Gillian's.

"I'd enjoy that," Gillian said.

"How does it fit in with your schedule tomorrow?" Laura asked.

"Perfect. I saved tomorrow to spend some time with you."

"Great. Then it's a date."

"Is ten o'clock okay?"

"Sounds good."

"I'll pick you up at your hotel at ten," Gillian said.

"Is the little VW bug I saw in the garage yours?" Laura asked.

"Yes, it is."

"I had one when I was in college. I loved it!" Laura smiled. "It'll be fun," she said, standing.

Dusty stood. "Do you want me to help you find the hotel?"

"No, darling. I'll be fine. I have directions, and it looks easy enough," she said.

Chapter Twenty-Nine

Laura was waiting in front of the hotel when Gillian pulled up. She wore white slacks, a teal silk blouse, and white with gold beaded high heel sandals. A large natural straw bag with huge colorful flowers completed her outfit. Gillian threw her purse in the backseat to make room for Laura to sit. Gillian wore khaki colored shorts with a red scooped neck styled knit T-shirt.

Gillian put the Bug into gear and headed to the first stop on their shopping trip of the bridal shops in the area. "Do you have something in mind you'd like me to wear to the wedding?" Laura asked.

"Samantha's dress is a dusty rose, so anything that won't clash with it is the only thing I can think of." Gillian stopped at a light in the intersection. "I want to thank you again for loaning your wedding dress to me, Laura. Is it okay I call you Laura?"

"You can call me whatever you feel comfortable with."

"It is the most beautiful dress I've even seen. I love it."

"I'm so glad. You are going to be a beautiful bride."

"The lady from my church who altered the dress called last night and said it's ready, so we can swing by and pick it up later."

"Wonderful."

"We'll go to David's Bridal first. Samantha got her dress there," Gillian said. "After lunch we can go to the Victorian Wedding Dresses."

"Have you found a veil or a hat to wear?"

"No. Not yet."

"The Victorian shop may be just the place to find one. If it's okay with you, I'd like to buy it for you," Laura said.

"You've already done so much by loaning me your wedding dress."

"I'd really like to. I've never had a daughter to buy things for."

Gillian glanced over at Laura, noticing her gaiety.

"Oh let's go there first...to the Victorian shop you mentioned. I can look for a dress and we can find you a veil or a hat." Laura sat on the edge of the seat, reminding Gillian of a school girl.

After parking the car, they walked into the Victorian store. Laura led the way and went directly to the section where veils and hats were displayed. "What do you think of this one?" she asked.

"It's beautiful."

Laura took it from the stand and gently placed it on Gillian's head. Standing behind her, she looked at Gillian's reflection in the mirror. "I think the shade will match the dress."

"Uh-huh." Gillian took it off. "It's beautiful, but not for me. It's over powering with so many large flowers and the beads hanging down are too much. It's not only over powering for me, it will take away from the dress too."

"You're right. It's much too fussy. You need something more complementary to your figure and one you'll feel comfortable wearing," Laura said. She picked up a veil with a single rose. "What do you think about this one?"

Gillian took the veil from Laura and tried it on. "Do you know what Dusty is planning to wear to the wedding?"

"He told me he's going to wear black trousers and a frock coat."

"Really?"

Gillian nodded. And a top hat too."

"I can't wait to see him!" Laura glanced around the store. "I'm going over to the dress section." Laura strolled away while Gillian continued to try on veils and hats.

After trying on several dresses, Laura emerged from the dressing room, smiling. She waltzed toward Gillian, sitting on a setae. Laura twirled around. "What do you think?" She wore a champagne-colored sheer silk dress with a handkerchief hemline. The beaded detail of a delicate design, also on the matching jacket, fit her perfect size ten shapely figure. Gillian thought the genteel, elegant dress was made for her.

"I like it."

"So do I." Laura stifled a giggle. "Did you find something?"

"I think so, but first I want to know what you think."

"I'll get dressed and be right with you." Laura returned to the dressing room.

Within minutes, Laura appeared from behind the dressing room curtain carrying the dress on a hanger. "Let's see what you've chosen."

Gillian took the simple Victorian hat with the wide brim from the display and placed it on her head at an angle.

"It's ideal." Laura clasped her hands and held them to her chest. "The perfect choice."

Climbing into Gillian's VW bug, Laura said, "I'm ready for some lunch, how 'bout you?"

"There's a nice restaurant at Fashion Island."

"Sounds good to me."

After being seated at the restaurant they both ordered Shrimp Louise's and iced tea. Gillian laid her napkin across her lap. *My first impression of Dusty was wrong. I pray my impression of his mother is right. She's like the mother I always dreamed about when I played with my imaginary family in my doll house. She's loving, kind, friendly, wise, and beautiful too -- a real lady.*

"I'm so delighted you and Dusty have found each other," Laura said. She sipped her water. "I'm so sorry about what you're going through with the house situation."

"It's more than disappointing, for sure." Gillian paused. "There isn't anything I can do about it, so I'm trying to let it go." Her fork hovered over her salad. "I am glad our wedding will be there though. I plan to think of it as a chapter of my life ending and another beginning."

"It's bittersweet for you...sort-of like when I gave birth to Dusty and was grieving the death of Dusty's father at the same time. He died only weeks before in a tragic car accident. During that time, I shed tears of sorrow and tears of joy."

It appeared to Gillian Laura wanted to talk, so she listened.

"Do you mind if I talk about Dusty's father?"

"Not at all. In fact, I'd like to know about him. Dusty doesn't talk about him."

"It's probably because he never knew him. He only had pictures of him and what I told him about his father." Laura blotted her mouth with the linen napkin. "Dusty looks like his father, but that is the only thing they have in common. Rick was an extravert whereas Dusty is an introvert. And Rick was a risk taker. Like his father, Rick was a doctor and everyone loved him."

"Rick's father was Pop?"

"Yes. When Rick died, Pop gladly took on the male influence in Dusty's life. He never missed a Little League game or a school program, even with a busy practice. From the day Dusty was born, Pop was a huge part of Dusty's life. He was the one who delivered Dusty. Did Dusty tell you?"

"No. He told me he had a special relationship with his grandfather and they did all kinds of things together." Gillian sipped her iced tea.

"They sure did. Pop took Dusty to Lake Tahoe in the winter and taught him how to ski. And I'm sure he's told you about Pop teaching him how to surf."

Gillian smiled and nodded.

"He took Dusty to the San Francisco Opera," Laura said. "Sometimes they would even let me tag along with them."

"Does Dusty like opera?" Gillian asked.

"I don't think so. It's more like he tolerates it. We both know he took to surfing." Laura smiled.

"Yes. We do."

"I'm going on and on."

"It's okay, really. I want to know more."

128

Laura reflected. "After Dusty was born, he was my whole life. He was a sweet little boy, never rambunctious. He liked to do quiet things like play with his Legos and army men. He loved books and I read to him every night. When he was older, he helped his grandfather build a tree house in our backyard. He would sit up there for hours. I think that's when he realized he liked to work with his hands and build things."

Gillian felt comfortable being with Laura. She felt a bond with her she had never felt with her own mother, and she wanted to hear everything about Laura, and Pop, and Dusty.

Laura went on, "I was never interested in dating. No one could take the place of Rick and I had Dusty." She took a breath. "It wasn't until Dusty graduated from high school and started college that he said to me, 'Mom, don't you think it's about time you thought about yourself?' He knew, and I did too. It was time for me to move on, so I started going out, first with friends, as a fifth wheel, so to speak. And there were some matchmaking attempts by friends. They'd invite a friend to dinner for me to meet. It was Matt who I had worked with for years and I'd known his wife before she passed away. Matt and I had had a working relationship and a friendship too. I knew Matt would be there for me if I ever needed him. Of course, both Dusty and I always had Pop until a couple of years ago." Laura looked with nostalgia. "What began as a working relationship and a friendship turned into something more and Matt and I were married a year ago."

Gillian only half listened. She was thinking about what Laura had said about Dusty going to college. He had never told her he went to college.

"I really have bended your ear now."

"Dusty went to college?" Gillian asked.

"Yes. He graduated from Stanford."

Gillian stiffened. *What else hasn't Dusty told me?*

"I can't believe my rudeness. I'd like to know more about you. Dusty has told me a great deal, but I want to know everything." Laura nodded toward the dessert tray with a selection of goodies including a delightfully gooey slice of chocolate cake. "How about a dessert?"

"I'm stuffed. I couldn't eat another thing."

"Neither could I, really. It's just... I love chocolate." Laura smiled. "Let's get one, and you can tell me all about yourself."

Chapter Thirty

While Dusty drove Laura back to the hotel, Gillian lay on one of the twin beds in Samantha's bedroom, watching her iron a dress. "I'm not sure I trust Dusty," Gillian said.

"What do you mean you don't trust him?" Samantha asked as she set the iron at the end of the ironing board and gave Gillian her undivided attention.

"He never told me he graduated from Stanford."

"Is that why you've been moping around all evening?" Samantha put the pressed dress on a hanger and hung it in the closet.

"Don't you think it's something he would tell his fiancé?" Without waiting for an answer Gillian continued, "Maybe I'm jumping out of the frying pan into the fire. I feel like he's deceived me."

"You've got cold feet, that's all. Lots of people get cold feet before they get married."

Gillian was silent, thinking, mulling everything over in her mind.

Samantha began, "I know I'm a flirt..."

"What does you being a flirt have to do with what I'm talking about?"

"You didn't let me finish. I'm also good at gut feelings. The church would call it discernment. So what if he didn't tell you he graduated from Stanford? Maybe he went to college to please someone else. Or maybe it's something he wants to forget. I don't know. I do know he is rock solid and he adores you."

"I'm going for a walk," Gillian said heading toward the bedroom door.

"Wait! I'll go with you."

"I want to be alone."

Taking a jacket from one of the pegs in the laundry room, Gillian pulled it on and walked out of the house and down the stairs to the beach below. She plowed through the sand, her head down. After a while, she looked straight ahead and whispered a prayer, "Dear Lord, I need to know that I'm doing the right thing. I need to feel your peace. Because I've been so hurt by my mother, that I don't trust anyone. And I'm afraid that Dusty hasn't been honest with me. Please help me and my confusion. Give me your peace that I'm doing the right thing in marrying Dusty. Help me to know which way to turn." She walked and walked and walked.

When she strolled back toward the house, Dusty met her halfway along the beach. He slid his arm around her waist and walked beside her. "Are you getting cold feet?" he asked.

"Did you talk to Samantha?"

"She told me you were upset." He pulled her closer. "So, are you getting cold feet?"

"I'm not sure."

They walked in silence.

"How come you never told me you graduated from Stanford?" She asked.

"It just never came up." Their strides mirrored each other like synchronized swimmers. "I didn't think it was important. If I thought it was, I would have told you." He stopped and held her at arm's length facing him. "Gillian, you need to trust me. I would never, never do anything to hurt you, ever. After God, you are the most important person in my life and I would die for you. Don't you know that?" He had tears in his eyes.

She moved into his arms and rested her head on his chest.

After returning to the house, she leaned against him as they sat together on the chaise lounge on the patio. "If you want to reschedule the wedding, I'll understand," he said.

"All the arrangements have been made."

"They can be cancelled."

"No." She sat up and turned to face him. "I know I still have some issues to work through...with the help of New Hope. I've already made some progress, especially with my anorexia."

"You sure have." He pinched her waist, only finding skin to squeeze.

She turned and nestled back down against him, enjoying a comfortable silence with only the rumble of the surf below and a gentle breeze.

As she rested against him with his arms around her, he put his lips against her hair and breathed in its fragrant scent. "I do have something I need to tell you, but it has to do with my wedding gift to you...so you will have to wait a little longer. Do you trust me enough to wait?"

"Yes, Dusty, I trust you. I can wait."

The day before the wedding, a frenzy of activity whirled around the beach house on Cliff Drive. Gillian, Samantha, Laura, and some of the ladies from the church cleaned and decorated the house. While the women readied the inside of the house for guests, Josh took a day off to help Dusty mow and edge, making the yard look like a park. When everything was done, Laura and the church ladies left and Samantha and Josh took off together to do some last minute errands.

Holding hands, Gillian and Dusty strolled around the yard then gazed at the house they had restored together. For Gillian, it had begun as a tribute to her grandmother. She now knew that for Dusty it had been a time of working through his own grieving process for his grandfather. While working side by side, they had fallen in love. Not only was the house restored, but Gillian was on the road to restored health, and the perfect figure she once had. And, through Gillian's witness, Dusty came to know the Lord as his personal Savior.

"We did it!" Dusty said, squeezing her hand.

"It's more beautiful than I remember. I wonder if this is how it looked when it was new and Gram first saw it as a young bride."

Dusty looked down at her and saw her smile turn to a frown. "What's the matter?" he asked.

"I'm worried about when the new owners are going to call, all the packing and moving, and getting ready for school to start. It's overwhelming."

"Don't worry," Dusty said assuredly. "Didn't Pastor Mike say in one of his sermons something about not being anxious... and how God takes care of the birds... and you are of more value than they are?"

Gillian sighed deeply. "I know the verse." She smiled. "You've grown a lot in your faith."

"Like a sponge. I'm like a sponge soaking it all up." He picked her up and twirled her around. Setting her down, he said seriously, "I know you trust God." His eyes held hers. "You can trust me too." He bent down and kissed her.

Pulling away to catch her breath, she said, "Okay. You've convinced me." She smiled. "Now convince me more."

Chapter Thirty-One

Gillian and Dusty's wedding day dawned warm with an ocean breeze, making it a perfect temperature for a perfect day. A harpist sitting off to the side, near the rose garden, played the hymns which Gillian had chosen -- the same ones Gram had hummed while doing her chores around the house. The wedding guests arrived and walked under the rose-covered arched trellis and on to the lawn area where white folding chairs faced the beautiful blue Pacific.

Dressed in a long, elegant, dusty rose-colored bridesmaid dress with spaghetti straps, Samantha peered out the upstairs window. "It's filling up. My parents are here and Josh's parents just arrived."

Gillian stood at the long mirror, taking one last look. "You ready, Sam?"

Samantha came away from the window and joined Gillian.

"Before we go downstairs, I want to give you something." Gillian took a gold locket from the gift box. Opening it, she showed Samantha the photos inside, one of her and one of Gillian. "Thank you for being my friend all these years. I know I haven't been the greatest friend to you these last few months, but you stuck by me even when I was a--"

Samantha interrupted, "Don't make me cry, Gilly." Embracing each other, Samantha continued, "Thank you. I'll always treasure it."

Holding their bouquets, they checked their reflections in the mirror one last time. "Let's go," Gillian said. They descended the stairs and once outside Gillian put her arm through the crook of Samantha's. They met Josh, Laura, and Matt standing near by the trellis.

"Wow, Gilly! You look beautiful," Josh said, kissing her on the cheek.

Gillian received hugs from Laura and Matt as they echoed Josh's sentiments.

"Thanks," Gillian said, and then she looked out toward the horizon and saw Dusty standing with his strong hands clasped in front of him, waiting -- waiting for her.

The wedding procession music began and Josh ushered Laura down the aisle with Matt following, then he took his place at Dusty's side as his best man.

Samantha squeezed Gillian's hand before she walked down the aisle, leaving Gillian standing alone under the trellis. As Mendelssohn's "Wedding March" heightened, everyone stood and Gillian stepped forward and walked toward her groom, her eyes only on him, and his on her.

Holding his Bible, Pastor Mike began, "This is a joyous occasion. Marriage must have been very important to our Lord, because He performed his first miracle at a wedding. After talking with Gillian and Dusty, it's probably a miracle this wedding is even taking place."

A low rumble of laughter rippled through the guests seated behind the couple.

"Dusty told me recently he had no intensions of getting married when he moved here a few months ago. He said he came for the waves. He didn't expect God, or Gillian, to capture his heart. In fact, he told me when he first met her he didn't even like her." Pastor Mike paused for only a moment then continued. "To be fair, Gillian said when she first met Dusty she thought 'he's just another surfer', but God works in mysterious ways."

He paused, looking at Gillian, then at Dusty. "God brought this couple together and they are about to embark on a lifetime adventure together with God. They believe with God they can face anything."

"Dusty, God's word teaches that as the husband of Gillian, you are to be the leader of the home you are now establishing. To be worthy of that leadership you are to love her as Jesus loved the church and gave His life for it. As He is our Savior, you are to be her protector and defender. As Jesus is our provider, you are to provide for Gillian and be faithful to her showing the same mercy you hope to receive from God, in all seasons and circumstances as long as you both shall live."

Pastor Mike turned to Gillian. "As Dusty is to be the spiritual head of your new home and so represent Christ, so you will be the heart of this new home and so represent the church. Submit yourself to Dusty and lovingly uphold his leadership and authority in your home and in the church. Your beauty, talents, skills, and abilities should be a delight to Dusty. Do not neglect yourself or his desires, but trust the Lord to give you the grace to please your husband. Do not forget Dusty will need your devotion whether in prosperity or poverty, sickness or health, whether he is worthy or unworthy, as long as you both shall live."

"Dusty and Gillian will now share the vows they've written to each other," Pastor Mike said.

Gillian and Dusty faced each other. He rubbed his thumbs over Gillian's hands as she spoke. "Dusty, you have taught me how to have fun. I believe God's desire for me is abundant life, and He knew I needed you. You've taught me how to have a more abundant life. You've shown me how to have fun, to laugh at myself, and to share God's joy with others. I promise to hold you, Dusty, as the one true love of my life on this day and forever. As we stand before God, I solemnly vow to spend each day of my life with you and only you by my side."

"Gillian, you are everything and more than I could ever imagine in someone. I want to spend the rest of my life with you as my wife. Your love for God and the personal relationship you have with Him was what I was missing. You were instrumental in my coming to know Jesus as my personal Lord and Savior. I love you. I respect you. I love your laugh. You complete me. You are my soulmate and I plan to provide for you and protect you. I will never leave you. I will devote each day to learning how to better serve Christ with you. We shall create a life together which will honor God. I want to grow old with you at my side."

Placing the ring on her finger and gazing into her eyes he said, "I, Dusty, offer you, Gillian, my hand in marriage before God and these present. I promise to honor, love unconditionally, and cherish each moment we have together. I will always respect you, your goals, and look forward to being a part of those from now and until the end of time. For this is my solemn vow."

They turned to face Pastor Mike as he asked, "Dusty, will you have Gillian to be your wedded wife to live together after God's ordinance in the holy estate of matrimony? Will you love her, comfort her, and keep her in sickness and in health and forsaking all others, keep yourself only unto her as long as you both shall live?"

"I will."

"Gillian, will you have Dusty to be your wedded husband to live together after God's ordinance in the holy estate of matrimony? Will you love him and serve him, honor and keep him, in sickness and in health forsaking all others, keep yourself only unto him as long as you both shall live?"

"I will."

The harpist played "Ave Maria" as Dusty and Gillian stepped to the table with the white lace cloth. Gillian took the pink rose from the vase and Dusty took the white one. Together they stepped to where Laura sat and handed her the roses and kissed her cheeks. With tears of joy, Laura hugged them. Dusty and Gillian returned to the table and each poured their sand into the single clear container, uniting the white and black sand which represented their oneness.

Pastor Mike said, "Dusty and Gillian, by the power and authority vested in me as a minister of Jesus Christ and as your pastor and friend who loves you and prays God's best in your new life together, I now pronounce you husband and wife. Dusty, you may now kiss your bride."

Dusty grabbed Gillian around her waist and pulled her close. He kissed her passionately. When he finally released her, she had to catch her breath.

B J Bassett

Smiling, they turned to face their guests.

Pastor Mike said, "Family and friends it is with great pleasure and joy I present to you for the first time Mr. and Mrs. Dusty Bradshaw."

Chapter Thirty-Two

Dusty put his hand over his chest where the inside pocket of his jacket held his wedding gift to Gillian.

The ladies from the Little Chapel by the Sea brought huge bowls of food from the kitchen and placed them on long serving tables on the patio while the guests took their seats around decorated round tables. Gillian, Dusty, Josh, and Samantha joined Pastor Mike in the den, each signing their name in the appropriate place on the marriage certificate. "Let me be the first to congratulate you," Pastor Mike said, reaching out his hand to Dusty, and then hugging Gillian. Pastor Mike and Josh left to join the others, while Dusty and Gillian stayed back. "We'll catch up with you," Dusty said to Samantha.

"No way! You two have a lifetime together. Right now your guests and the photographer are waiting." Samantha grabbed Gillian's arm and pulled her toward the door.

Disappointed, Dusty said, "I guess it can wait until later."

Champagne glasses, filled with sparkling apple cider, were served.

Samantha tapped her glass to get everyone's attention. When it was silent, she cleared her throat. "I've known Gillian since kindergarten. We've been friends all through elementary school, middle school, high school, and college. Gillian has always been the leader in our friendship. She's been my example. She's been a friend to me through the good times and the bad." Her voice cracked. "I'd better stop 'cause I don't want my mascara to smear." She held up her glass. "Here's to Gillian and Dusty."

Josh had taken off his jacket, his rusty-colored hair slicked back. He held his glass in front of him. In his other hand he held a slip of paper with his toast written on it. "I'd like to make a toast." He cleared his throat, obviously trying to hold back the emotion he felt. "I've also known Gillian since kindergarten. She was the prettiest and sweetest girl in school and I fell in love with her then, and I still love her. We've always been close." He held his emotion in check by adding humor. "I'm the 'best man'. So why didn't I get the girl?"

Laughter filtered through the crowd.

"Seriously, Dusty is the real best man. When I first met him a year ago, he was someone to surf with. These last few months our friendship has grown, and I've found him to be a hard worker, a caring person, and a good friend." He took a deep breath. "About a month ago, Gillian told me how much she loved Dusty. She didn't have to tell me because it showed. Gillian's always had trouble hiding her feelings." He raised his glass in the air. "Here's to the prettiest and sweetest girl, and here's to the best man, Gillian and Dusty. May you always be as happy as you are today. And I hope you have oodles of kids."

Next Laura, with Matt at her side, stepped forward. She took the microphone from Josh. "I'm Dusty's mother. Dusty's father was killed in a car accident before Dusty was born, so I raised my son as a single parent. I'm very proud of him." She took a deep breath. "I believe his father is looking down on him today and he is proud of him too. Dusty is a wonderful son." She looked lovingly at him and Gillian. "Now I have a lovely daughter too. Gillian is everything, and more, than I ever dreamed a daughter could be. I am blessed." She paused, gaining composure. Matthew stood close by, supporting her in his quiet way. Laura continued, "Like Dusty's father, there are two others who are not with us in body today. They are with us in spirit. One of them is Gillian's grandmother and the other is Dusty's grandfather. Both of them were instrumental in the raising of the couple who stand before you today. I would like us to raise our glasses toasting Gillian and Dusty's happiness, and to the memory of Gram and Pop."

There were a few tears on their beautiful day -- tears for missed loved ones and tears of joy.

With the last of the guests gone, the Cape Cod beach house in Reagan Beach was dark except for a single light in the master bedroom. Gillian and Dusty, still in their Victorian wedding attire, sat side by side facing each other on the edge of the bed. "I wanted to give this to you earlier," Dusty said. He pulled the business size envelope from the inside pocket of his jacket and handed it to her.

Curious, Gillian slit the envelope open with her manicured nail. After unfolding the document, she read, "Deed". She looked quizzically at Dusty. "What's this?"

"It's the deed to the house."

Her eyes darted quizzically from the deed to Dusty. "I don't understand. I thought my mother sold the house."

"She did. I bought it... for you."

"How?"

"Pop made some good investments during his lifetime and he left everything to me."

"The house sold three weeks ago. Why didn't you tell me then?"

"Because I needed to make sure you were marrying me for the right reason. I needed to know you love me more than the house."

"Oh, Dusty, how could you ever think such a thing? I could never love anything more than I love you."

138

In unison, they stood facing each other holding hands. Dusty rubbed his thumbs back and forth over her hands.

She vowed, "No more secrets from each other from now on."

"I promise." He leaned down and kissed her inviting lips, a long lingering kiss. "Are you sorry we didn't go on a honeymoon?"

"There is no place I'd rather be than with you in this house." She turned her back to him, and with her hands she lifted her brunette curls from off her shoulders. "Mr. Bradshaw, will you please unbutton all these buttons for me."

"Yes, Mrs. Bradshaw. I'd be happy to." A gentle breeze fluttered the organdy curtains, and the surf rumbled below.

The End

Afterword

Although *Gillian's Heart* is fictional, Royal Family Kids' Camps (RFK) is an actual international organization. It was founded in 1985 by Wayne and Diane Tesch.

This innovative ministry offers training and resources for local churches to sponsor a 5-day summer camp for abused and neglected children of your area.

Working in cooperation with the state foster care agency, your church can make a lasting impact in the lives of some of the neediest children in your county!

For more information, see https.rfk.org.

About BJ Bassett

B. J. Bassett encourages others as an author, teacher and speaker.

Her books include a historical novel *Lily*; *Sweet Charity*; *A Touch of Grace—The G.R.A.C.E. Ministries Story*, and coauthor of *My Time with God* which sold 55,000 copies while in print.

She teaches writing workshops at Umpqua Community College in Roseburg, Oregon and at writer's conference. As a speaker for Stonecroft Ministries, she tells her story of rejection and acceptance, not only in life, but as a writer as well. She also offers book talks, including discussion questions and shares the journey—from the seed of an idea to a publisher book.

She enjoys reading, jigsaw puzzles, knitting, munching warm scones oozing with butter and strawberry jam and sipping earl grey tea. A native Californian, she now lives with her husband of 60 years in Roseburg, Oregon, where she wrote *Gillian's Heart*.

Made in the USA
Columbia, SC
12 October 2022